Journe

## ABOUT THE AUTHOR

Toby Litt was born in 1968. He is the author of *Adventures in Capitalism*, *Beatniks*, *Corpsing*, *deadkidsongs*, *Exhibitionism*, *Finding Myself*, *Ghost Story*, *Hospital* and *I play the drums in a band called* okay. In 2003, he was named one of Granta's Best of Young British Novelists. His website can be found at www.tobylitt.com

# Journey into Space

## TOBY LITT

PENGUIN BOOKS

PENGUIN BOOKS

Published by the Penguin Group
Penguin Books Ltd, 80 Strand, London WC2R ORL, England
Penguin Group (USA) Inc., 375 Hudson Street, New York, New York 10014, USA
Penguin Group (Canada), 90 Eglinton Avenue East, Suite 700, Toronto, Ontario, Canada M4P 2Y3
(a division of Pearson Penguin Canada Inc.)
Penguin Ireland, 25 St Stephen's Green, Dublin 2, Ireland (a division of Penguin Books Ltd)
Penguin Group (Australia), 250 Camberwell Road, Camberwell, Victoria 3124, Australia
(a division of Pearson Australia Group Pty Ltd)
Penguin Books India Pvt Ltd, 11 Community Centre, Panchsheel Park, New Delhi – 110 017, India
Penguin Group (NZ), 67 Apollo Drive, Rosedale, North Shore 0632, New Zealand
(a division of Pearson New Zealand Ltd)
Penguin Books (South Africa) (Pty) Ltd, 24 Sturdee Avenue,
Rosebank, Johannesburg 2196, South Africa

Penguin Books Ltd, Registered Offices: 80 Strand, London WC2R ORL, England

www.penguin.com

First published 2009

1

Set in Monotype Janson
Typeset by Rowland Phototypesetting Ltd, Bury St Edmunds, Suffolk
Printed in England by Clays Ltd, St Ives plc

ISBN: 978–0–141–03971–8

www.greenpenguin.co.uk

Penguin Books is committed to a sustainable future
for our business, our readers and our planet.
The book in your hands is made from paper
certified by the Forest Stewardship Council.

I

'Describe,' said Celeste, and so August began with 'It is gentle and warm and soft and –' And he ran out of adjectives. He rebegan with, 'It is like being touched by the softest thing that has ever touched you but also like not being touched at all. It is a paradox.' *Paradox* was too hard a word, though – it was hard to describe. 'It is hard to describe,' he said, 'but it is softer than the word *paradox*. That sounds too harsh and makes it sound too complicated.' He was getting lost. 'I know I'm getting lost,' he said.

'No, you're doing very well,' Celeste said. 'I don't know if I could even begin to describe it.'

August was more than sure she could. 'You can try,' he said. 'I'll let you take over.'

'But not today,' she said. 'Today is for you. Keep going – keep describing how it would be, if it were.'

But there was no next sentence in August's mind – his eyes, he realized, were open: as if he might be able to catch sight of something earthly-ghostly in the darkness above. 'You can smell all the smells of the park all around you – the trees smell of . . .' This was atrocious; he knew nothing, really, about trees. He had been about to say *the trees smell of trees*. 'They smell of their colours, green for the leaves and dark brown for the bark of the trunk.' He knew *bark* and *trunk*; he did know something. The image in his head was that of an oak tree – he recognized it from one of the tattered picture books he'd been given as a child and had several years ago been forced to pass on: a green cloud shape stuck on top of another shape like a foot seen from the front, in brown: *foliage* – a word he had recently learnt from *it*, a word he had wanted to display for Celeste, but now the moment was missed. Then he had an inspiration: 'All around you, you can hear the breeze brushing against the leaves of the trees.' He had studied equations for turbulence; he knew about this solidly. 'The air is becoming chaotic. Straight lines, if you could see them, are twisted and split and thrown back upon themselves. The sound you hear is the sound of those lines. But it is a soft sound, I think. Not violent.' Celeste, he knew, had also studied the equations, had sat beside him in class, which made this part of the describing seem suddenly pointless.

'That's beautiful,' Celeste said. There could be no doubt of it: she was crying.

'The grass underneath you is –'

'Enough,' she said. 'Enough-enough. Just let me *be* there for a little while. You've taken me. I'm here. I want to stay.'

August, still flat on his back, closed his eyes again and tried to untense all the muscles in his body: he wasn't there, where he'd described: Central Park, New York. He was the artist and had transported another person, but he remained excluded from the world of his words.

Perhaps next time. Perhaps when Celeste did the describing for him. Of one thing he was now certain: If this were to continue as it had begun, he must find out as much as he could about the sensations of Earth. He must develop a vocabulary; one he was totally in control of, so that he was able to use any part, even when lost in panic – if the weather-moment required. He would ask *it* to show him what to read.

Beside him, Celeste gave a small sigh; she seemed to exhale other air – cooler than it went in, fresher, greener.

I need to know about Nature, August thought.

'Describe,' August said, the following year, and Celeste replied by saying, 'It is so beautiful, just the idea of it – something which is *there* but which you can't see, which touches you but leaves nothing behind. If anything, it *takes* – tiny flakes, tiny particles of us. I know we have lots of things here that are like that in some way, blowy things. But they can't really be the same, or anything close, can they? It's silent, unless it's coming out of a vent. It doesn't make any sound itself, crossing empty spaces high up between buildings or between trees – it only gains a voice when, as you once said, turbulence is suggested to it, created within it, by the edges of an object – the cornice of a building, say, or a hedge.' August was overwhelmed by the idea of *cornice* and *hedge* – and even more so by the fact that Celeste had used these words. He knew what they meant, just about, but in her saying of them she had put the exact-crisp shapes of them in his mind. Now they hung above him in the flickering dark of the tennis courts. 'I remember you did a wonderful describing of Central Park, of us just lying beneath the trees one sunny day in July or June.

All this breeze of mine, the whole wall-like force of it, well, it hits this tree and it is cut into tiny twirling ribbons of turbulence – all going in a million different directions, so complex that no person could ever map it or draw it. Or understand it. And it is this which creates the sound of the breeze. Can you hear it?'

'Yes,' August said, and he could. Celeste continued anyway. 'This is an inhuman sound, even though it is frequently likened to a voice, or to voices. We must never forget our distance; although it is *like* something here, it isn't really that thing at all. It is often compared to the sound of many people speaking quietly at once – of a whole vast crowd whispering; sometimes louder over here, sometimes quieter everywhere. But we will never hear the sound of a thousand people, and we will never hear the wind blowing, so we will never know.'

Celeste was often like this: rigorous to the point of destroying the effect she had only just created. August could have predicted what was to follow. With his eyes still closed, he could hear Celeste breathing in, tucking herself up, rocking herself back and then rolling up into a cross-legged crouch before standing fluidly-fully and walking away. The tennis courts were so quiet, apart from the everywhere-hum, that the sound of each of these movements was distinct. 'I'm not happy,' said Celeste. 'I'm just not good enough – and it's ruining it for you, and that's ruining it for me.' After a year of good research, August knew quite well what *ruins* were. He liked the idea of ruins.

Celeste walked until she was perhaps ten metres away, then said, 'Perhaps we should abandon it. All it does is cause pain. Is torture what we want it for? Do we dislike ourselves that much?' These questions weren't for August, and he knew better than to try and answer them. If the moment went well, Celeste might make one of her magnificent speeches, saving everything that had almost been lost with a wordstorm so perfect it couldn't have been achieved without the preceding upset. But today, it seemed, wasn't to be one of those resurrected days. 'I'm stopping,' she said. 'I have no more.'

August told her not to worry and, in a no less agile manner than Celeste, flipped to his feet. He wanted to comfort her, but he knew he would have to do this with words only. They had stopped touching when they stopped playfighting, maybe two years ago, when they had their thirteenth birthdays. 'You'll feel better about it next time,' said August. 'What you did was beautiful. I was entirely there. It felt –'

'You were?' Celeste asked.

'Entirely,' said August. 'I could feel the whole world all around me, in every direction.'

Celeste was silent for a short while, then said, 'I haven't felt that in months. It's not your fault. You've been marvellous – some of the best detailed describing ever. I don't know if I'll ever forget last month, standing on that exposed headland just after the April shower had passed – with the wonderful detail of the raindrops still clinging to the petals of the sea-pinks and other clifftop plants. It's not your fault,' she said, a second time. 'But I seem to be dying.' Again, August knew better than to ask her to explain. 'My capacity is dying. It was so easy, once. All I needed was a new word, and I was back. Now, I can be there, but it's like I'm just a dead person laid out in the grass – a dead person who's still alive. I can see, and my other senses work, but nothing really penetrates. Cold isn't cold like it should be. Even that frost you did, last week, which was very beautiful, it didn't chill me like it should have.'

Without saying anything further, they began to walk to the door. Although the tennis courts were almost completely dark, they knew their way unthinkingly. The one remaining fluorescent tube ticked on and off with a slowly slowing rhythm – sometimes minutes passed before it came back on, leading them to think it had died completely.

At least a decade had passed since anyone had used the courts for their original purpose – not since the last of the tennis balls had perished completely, so much that it hardly bounced any more; and then, with a final winning smash, had popped like a puffball in a cloud of rubbery dust. (This was preserved for the future in a test-tube.)

Since that last game, the courts – all eight of them, two by four – had remained almost entirely unvisited. Hardly surprising, because they were on a rarely needed deck.

It was only during one of the fourth-generation-children's epic games of chocolate-hunt that Celeste and August, together as always, had discovered the existence of the courts. Ever since, the courts were where they had gone when they wanted the illusion of privacy – although, at the start, so used were they to being watched, they didn't even have an idea of the concept. The courts could still be seen through *it*, and anyone could have tracked them down. But because of the dark in there, they were unseen except for determined looking – in other words, if someone turned on the infra-red or heat-detection.

By general agreement, parents did not spy upon their children past the age of eleven. There was very little they could get up to that was dangerous; *it* was aware of where they were and what they were doing at all times. Lying in the dark and talking did not merit an alarm or an alert.

Outside the door to the courts, they separated – Celeste turning right, August going left; and from here, each of the cousins made their way to a different elevator, along deep corridors. There were no portholes this far inside the ship, and so no chance of seeing anything other than metal and illumination.

The lights on these decks, both overhead and at ankle level, came on as they approached and went off almost as soon as they had passed – a saving of energy and precious filaments. It had been another of their childhood games, to try to outpace the lights, but, of course, it couldn't be done; *it*'s reactions and anticipations were faster than any child's. The most one could hope to achieve was to be slightly forward of the exact centre of the bubble or tube of light.

As they walked away from one another, they hardly noticed where they were; for Celeste and August, the UNSS *Armenia* had neither glamour nor grace. It was disgusting to them quite how well they knew it – all the accessible areas, at least. As adolescents, they now slunk down the same corridors they had once crawled along or raced through shouting lo-lo-lo! When they came to a particular door, they knew exactly the direction in which it opened, the resistance it was likely to give. Occasionally, maintenance lubricated the stiff or tightened the loose, but most of the time their environs offered Celeste and August no surprises, only a time-depth of mechanical and severely limited, and limiting, knowledge. If they had been on Earth, anywhere but in a prison, they would have sense-learnt paths and streets, beaches and fields, rockfaces and deserts. Instead, they knew corridor P-31 as the place where Celeste had pulled down Australia's pants so everyone saw his private parts. They knew that a mysterious smell of almonds or nuts of some sort came from under the cabin door of Mrs Woods, the last-surviving first-generationer.

The exterior was no better. Although none of the children, nor, in fact, the adults were aware of it, the vessel had been based by its designer upon the humped curve of *Arion ater agg*, commonly known as the large black slug. But despite the fact that their recognition of this could only possibly have been intuitive, both Celeste and August developed early on a sense of the vessel's essential sluggishness. It was not slow – at the time of its launch, the *Armenia* had been one of the ten fastest machines ever constructed. However, propulsion technology back on Earth was developing exponentially, and a large unmanned transporter, intended to resupply them a couple of years after they arrived on the destined planet, and which itself had set off a decade after they had, was now due to overtake them and arrive there a full generation ahead: it seemed quite possible, if things continued as they were, that their descendants would arrive on a partially colonized world. They would appear as, quite hilariously, a blast from the past; their equipment outmoded and unnecessary, their training and protocols redundant: more likely to be viewed as a drain on resources than a contribution to the new life. Still, they had to complete the journey; and, by most standards, one twentieth the speed of light was an incredible velocity. But space travel *wasn't* – *wasn't* travel; the reality of it being that there was no experience to have: the ship could quite as easily have been sitting in a purpose-built hangar in Florida, and the crew – as long as the window-simulations were good enough – would never have known the difference. Gravity was kept to 90 per cent of that on Earth, acclimatizing everybody to conditions on a planet they would never live to see. The vessel had made no discernible movement in over two decades. Among the youngest members of the crew, there was absolutely no sense of physical motion. This had consequences. One or two of the older children were reassured rather than upset by the total lack of events – and these tended to become hysterical whenever an older crew-member died. When the suicide occurred, the body had kept pace with the vessel for quite some time. Before they were pulled away, several children – among them Astra (later to become August's mother) but not Stella (later to give birth to Celeste) – had spotted it, and had waved happily and then frantically at the unresponsive woman. There was no such thing as an accident; why shouldn't Margaret take a walk outside, without a suit? The children asked and were told. The facts came as quite a shock to them. This was not unusual (though, in this case, it was unusually extreme).

To each growing child, there came the inevitable moment of devastation, when they finally understood where they lived, and where – yet more dismayingly – they had and would have no choice *but* to live. Up until a certain age, all the soft-edged, covers-missing books they lettered from and all the tattered toys they inherited were suggestive of the animals and countries of Earth; some children, as a result, became obsessed with the naturalistic extremities of Africa, lions, elephants, rhinoceroses, antelopes; others with the tigers of China or the polar bears of the Arctic; or, like Celeste and August, the whales and dolphins and sharks of the seven seas. Around five years of age, however, their moment came, and they realized that they were doomed to live and die in a tigerless, rhino-bereft, dolphin-free place. Some reacted to this by abandoning all interest in Earth lifeforms, others, such as Celeste's younger brother, found their obsession intensified. (His was for birds.) The cousins' moment came unusually early. They were found, aged two and a half, staring bleakly not through the main observation window, which faced forwards, but out of a small porthole that looked back in the direction from whence the vessel had come. How they had worked this out, no-one knew; what was certain was that they were crying, as if both their arms had been broken.

'What's wrong?' Celeste's mother had asked, when

her daughter was carried squealing away from the starlit view and back to their quarters.

'I want my home,' said Celeste, very definitely. The ship, despite her never having lived anywhere else, was never going to be her home; she sensed, she knew. 'I want everything.'

'What do you mean?' her mother asked. But all the explanation of *everything* that Celeste would give was '*Every*-thing.'

August, to his mother, twin sister to Celeste's mother, was a little more forthcoming. 'We don't like Mission. We want some of the animals. We want a house with doors you can go in of and out of and in of again. We want a dog and a cat and a pig . . .'

Both mothers then tried, with some difficulty and, it has to be said, with deep feelings of ambivalence, if not hypocrisy, to persuade the children (and also themselves) that the *Armenia* was truly a wonderful place to live, despite the absence of almost everything their children's picture books had given them to expect.

'There are millions of children who will be sitting at home on Earth, one day, listening to what you are saying now, and thinking how silly you were being – thinking how much they'd really really like to swap places with you. And they've never seen an elephant or an I don't know a dolphin, either.' Not outside a zoo, she thought.

But even as she spoke, Astra felt again the sharp longing to which the disappointment of her own animal-disillusion had brought her.

The two sisters, Stella and Astra, met up later that

evening, when their children were asleep, if not truly comforted, to speak and be critical.

'Why didn't Control anticipate this?' Stella said, meaning Mission Control.

'It's the hardest thing,' Astra agreed, 'when we're all trying to keep thinking what we're doing here is a great thing. That we're lucky.'

'*Think how many children on Earth wish they were here, travelling on a real space vessel.*'

'That's what I said to him. That's the official line.'

'Did it work?'

'No. I don't think *Think how lucky you are* ever does with children. They just know they want something, and if they can't have it the world's unjust.'

'We don't have a world,' said Astra. 'That's why it's unjust.'

'Control must have thought of this,' said Stella. 'We brought them up almost entirely on a diet of cuddly things. Why weren't special books created, with galaxies and supernovas and all the wonderful things we've seen or are going to see?' She spoke with much bitterness and some guilt; *wonderful* came out as the opposite. For how, aged five, Stella had yearned for a kitten – one just like the picture she had ripped from the book and kept beneath her pillow; a white-yellow-gold-orange-haired marmalade kitten with a big happy-making face. She still wanted one, that was something this whole episode made her realize. She still felt where it would fit, on her lap.

Their conversation did not pass unobserved, and sessions with the onboard psychologists were booked for both of them; and also for their children.

Astra's feelings of resentment were fairly easily dealt with; perhaps because they were directed so straightforwardly at Mission, perhaps, also, because the animals she had herself fixated upon were already unreachable: dinosaurs – baby-stegosauruses, in particular – had been her childish obsession, and because they were, in a sense, twice removed, it hadn't been difficult for her to give up hopes of them altogether.

'It's natural there should be a period of grief,' said the psychologist to Stella. 'In a way it really is like a true kind of personal loss that we all of us feel, each in our own particular way.' Attempted sincerity made her sentence collapsingly long. 'We all experience it, you know, in one way or another. But it passes, eventually. Together, we can help you work it through.'

Stella said *yes*, and tried to make herself believe she agreed, as well; the kitten, however, remained – the kitten and the ache of her empty cuddle-space.

And even thirty-two years later, on the point of gentle death, Stella found that this feeling had not gone away – had, in fact, continued to strengthen, until it became one of the reasons she was so easy about passing. To die, she hoped, was to be surrounded by soft, purring fur.


'Describe,' said Celeste, and this time August began with, 'Rain doesn't just fall – it's important to remember that. Sometimes it is known to go sideways; for example, in a particularly strong wind. And if, like now, we are on the top of a ridge on a really blowy day, the rain coming sideways might even seem to be going upwards, if it is leaping over the crest.'

August was dissatisfied with himself and his describing – more than ever. He knew facts, and facts were all he knew. But when he spoke them, he couldn't stop them sounding like facts. When Celeste spoke, she somehow made them seem like experiences – and, because of this, she was able to take him there. Perhaps, August thought, I am too worried about being correct. If I completely invented the weather, I wouldn't have to be afraid of getting it wrong.

He needed to start speaking again; Celeste's breathing told him she was impatient. 'There are accounts of the unpleasantness of some episodes of rain' – bad, he thought, bad-bad – 'where the breeze blowing it coldly into the face makes it feel like the person is being spat upon – that the weather personally hates them, and wants to do this most insulting thing. In almost all cultures, just as in ours, spitting in someone's face is a terrible thing to do.'

Celeste said, 'Spit in my face.'

August found himself unable to react.

'Spit in my face,' said Celeste.

'No.'

'Please. I want you to.'

'But why?'

'I want to know what it feels like, for the rain.'

'No, you don't. It's more –'

'I've had enough of words. We've agreed –'

'It's more than that. You think you'll enjoy it.'

This brought Celeste to a pause. She recovered quite quickly, however. 'Well, I won't be able to tell until you've done it, will I? Come on. I don't want to have to do it myself – that would just be stupid.'

There was more silence; the darkness flickered.

'You're wrong,' August said. 'I never want to look back at my life and know I spat at someone.' He did not say, *Particularly you.*

'Even because they asked you to?'

August tried to find his arguments – he felt that he must have some. 'That doesn't make it any better. I'd still be the spitter. Years in the future, you could still say, *He once spat at me.*'

'And you can show people me asking.'

August realized he had introduced an audience of unborn judges.

'But that's an explanation.' His voice rang off the walls of the tennis courts. 'The fact is, I did it – I was able to do it. People will only care about that. And the people who'll watch on Earth.'

They had propped themselves up on their elbows to have this discussion-not-argument. Now they lay back down and stared again towards where the ceiling was – each listening to the other's breathing, for clues.

'The rain gets heavier,' Celeste said, assumingly. 'It falls straight down, without deviating in any direction – although there is a slight breeze. We are sheltered a little, by the wall of stone you invented. Keep going.'

August was angry. For the first time, he wanted to describe badly, so as to frustrate Celeste.

'Writers sometimes speak of this kind of rain as coming down in sheets. Often, when there is a little wind, a rippling effect is visible in thick-falling downpours, and this must remind people of bedsheets, when they are hanging up. That is probably where it started.

Curtains are also sometimes mentioned, although this must be for thicker rain. Curtains, as you know, are used to cover windows on the inside – to stop people from looking in and seeing what's going on.'

'Don't patronize me.'

August continued. 'They can be made of many sorts of material, curtains, so this comparison – rain like curtains – could mean many different things. Net-curtains were notoriously used in England for spying through – it was easy to see out of a house but hard to see in. I think it was just about possible, though. If you got close. And velvet curtains keep heat inside when Winter cold is trying to drag it out. Curtains suggest an obstruction to vision whereas sheets, even though you can't really *see* through the fabric of cotton, suggest something more permeable to the eye.'

'Stop it,' said Celeste. August knew she meant the being annoying, not the describing. They were so familiar with one another's nuances.

He changed, for her. The ridiculousness of the curtains, so unhelpful, had rid him of his anger.

'We are lying in a strong, steady downpour of cold rain. The sky above us is without a hint of blue. It is many clouds that have become one single, solid, horizon-to-horizon cloud. This is white in colour but white that has been tainted with grey – made grubby by darkness. Each drop comes too fast for us to track it with our eyes; we can't pick them out, one by one, against the background of the sky. They are trans-parent –'

'That's enough,' Celeste said. 'I'm leaving.' But she did not move.

August waited. Celeste's breathing was not completely in her control. It was passionate.

'Of course they're *transparent*,' said Celeste, 'they're *water*.'

'It is easier to see rain when looking sideways through it than when looking up into it.'

When Celeste didn't respond, August stood up. 'All I'm saying is, with the light-source behind them, and their only change a slight increase in size, and maybe a deviation from the vertical, that when you stare up into raindrops, you don't really see them.'

The light flickered on. August could see exactly how Celeste lay, at his feet – angry relaxation.

'Plus the fact,' he added, 'that it's falling in your eyes, blinding you.'

And then, without thinking why he was doing it, he bent down and spat gently into her face.

When they returned this time from the tennis courts, Celeste and August noticed a general mood of celebration: people hugged as they passed in corridors, asking one another nonsensical questions, 'Have you heard? It's great news, isn't it?' *Nonsensical* because, if there was anything to be heard, people – people apart from Celeste and August – would have checked with *it* already, and be aware of exactly the same information as everybody else.

'Yes, it's wonderful, isn't it?' said Celeste, in reply to Australia, one of their contemporaries: Australia, who aspired to becoming Captain, but who, because of Celeste and August's actions, would never do so. Australia seemed more than content with Celeste's answer, so the two of them repeated it, parodically, to whomever else addressed them.

'Such wonderful news.'

'The news couldn't be more wonderful, could it?'

Celeste and August separated outside the door to her apartment. 'Yesterday,' she whispered into August's ear, as the last thing. *Yesterday*, meaning *tomorrow*, one of their communicative opposites.

As soon as August entered his own family's apartment, August's father, the vessel's First Officer, was upon him, attempting to explain exactly what had happened.

'What has happened is, they've signed a very important treaty – to do with Jerusalem. There's been a huge historical problem between the –'

August knew very little about Jerusalem and its significance, deliberately. Negotiations towards this treaty, whatever it was, had been in progress for most of his conscious life – serving only to render him (and Celeste) radically disinterested in the subject. August's attitude was a great annoyance to his father, who had tried time and again to impress upon him how important this treaty might prove to be. Jerusalem, so he believed, was the fount from which flowed all the pollutants of the world.

'Really?' said August. 'That's wonderful,' and then headed towards his room.

'This is one of the most important days of our lives,' said his father. 'And you won't even acknowledge it.'

As events proved, he was not wrong. And August, looking back in old age, would feel guilty at not having been able to share his father's huge and, so it turned out, illusory optimism.

The treaty, of course, hadn't been signed that day, but about two years before – it was just that communication between Earth and the ship now took that long. A continuous stream of information was aimed directly at *it*, but as the years passed this became more and more out of date. Congratulations were intermittently received on the birth of infants who, by then, had grown old enough to understand most of the words being spoken. And the news-snippets the crew got from the relations their great-grandparents had left behind often proved to be inaccurate even as they were received: the recently married were already divorced, the convalescent had died. Those following soap operas had to wait for longer and longer periods of time before the entirety of the next episode arrived. Games, although still played, were done so in the annoying knowledge that they were already outdated. Most people lost interest in anything resembling real-time experience of life on Earth. Instead, they found areas of historical specialization to enjoy. It was more satisfying to become expert in the culture of a particular period than to try to stay hip to the mutating fashions of twenty-five months ago. Mozart was complete, in as far as all the extant recordings, both audio and audiovisual, of all his known works were available via *it*. August's father was an enthusiast of Napoleon before 1812. His mother knew a lot about the suffragette movement of the early twentieth century. Some general interest in Earth was stirred, now and again, by a major scientific discovery or environmental disaster. Otherwise, the insular culture of the vessel was *it*.

'Describe,' said August, and Celeste said nothing – nothing for a very long time. Then she said, 'I have no ideas.' She said, 'I have nothing.'

'Of course you do,' said August. 'Begin with where we are. It'll go from there. It always does.' *With you*, he wanted to say. *With you but not with me.*

'We are on top of the hill. Beside us is a wall – the familiar wall. The one you built for us, so we would have something concrete to begin with. But it's not concrete, ha ha ha. It's gravel-rock from the surrounding landscape. It fits. I hate this wall. You did well to build it. I can see it so clearly. The beautiful blacks and greys. I'm sorry. I hate it.'

'It's not there any more,' said August. 'It's gone. Just a natural hilltop. It's gone.'

'No. It hasn't. It's here, and it stays here.'

'Not if you don't want it to.'

'Just because I hate something doesn't mean it doesn't have a right to exist.'

August said, 'I thought that was the whole point. And, anyway, it's just a wall – walls don't have rights.'

'This one does. If it wasn't there, I'd be in trouble every time. It has earned its existence, so it has rights.'

August took a relax-breath. 'We don't have to if you don't want to.' He meant describe; go.

'I want to,' Celeste said. 'I really want to – it's just, I can't. We are here. There is some weather.' She made a sound, halfway between *baah* and *bleurgh*.

'Be quiet,' said August. And, to his surprise, she was.

August lay there, distressed. Celeste seemed to have absented herself, immediately, although he could feel beside him the body-warmth of her. (The tennis courts were quite cold.) He wondered whether he should start speaking, begin a new describe. But she might not even hear him, so far off into the negative space of her own self-obsession was she. Traitorously, he felt that it would only have taken a very few words from her – '*There is a gentle south-westerly breeze*' or '*A light rain is beginning to fall*' – and he would have been transported. Just the tone of her voice was enough, these days; if she was confident in speaking, that confidence became the ground on which he lay, the sky that closed over him. Perhaps, he thought, we need a new start-point. It wasn't as if they knew nowhere else. Before settling upon the Lakes, as having the best and most interesting weather in the world, Celeste and August had experimented with dozens of climes and climates. After Central Park, they had treated one another to some of the most *outré* climatic conditions available to imagination. For him, she had created the plains of America and above them had sculpted high-piled clouds, lenticular and space-ship-seeming (like spaceships *should* have seemed). For her, he had narrated perilous sea-voyages, straight through the eyes of Florida-fated hurricanes. A few months of this meteorological baroque were enough, however. Within a year, they had settled down, some-what: drizzle, mizzle, fog, mist. But not all of the weathers they wanted were pleasant or comfortable. They were interested in whatever was possible. And so, in a couple of hours, one empty afternoon, they had endured a full rainy season in Wasgamuwa, Sri Lanka. Wishing, slightly later, to be sure they had experienced everything, they made a tour of the world's most piquant winds, from the enervating chinook to the mad-making mistral, from the bora – in both clear and dark forms – to the simoom which kills almost before it arrives. But eventually they had been drawn to New England, for the clarity of its quadruple seasons, and then to England, because it was the original. What transported them to the Lakes was Romantic Poetry; what made them stay was Dorothy Wordsworth and her Journal.

Not that their Lake District was historically accurate or geographically pedantic. They had allowed themselves to simplify and stylize things, somewhat. And thus their hill rose high above their lake – illuminated by it and reflected in it. All around, there were other hills, some higher, and other lakes, some deeper, but this hill was *the* hill, and this lake *the* lake. The lake had been influenced by, and yet was definitely *not*, Grasmere; the hill shared a few characteristics with Scafell Pike, though their identities were quite distinct. For a start, Celeste and August's planet was not Earth: it was smaller, cuter, city-free and unpopulated (apart from them, when they visited). Pollution, there, had never been known – and neither had war, adults, siblings or *it*. Sun and moon existed for them – two suns and two moons – but the landscape-light fell from elsewhere. Or rather, it did not fall but stood, shadowless or shadowy, as a mere fact of the place; the place which needed light to be seen, to be seeable. When necessary, it could coalesce into effects, mimic sunset or moonrise, but these were the issue of desire and not orbit. This was their made place, and both within it had always found a home. Until now.

Eventually, August heard from Celeste's breathing that she had fallen into an almost-sobbing form of sleep. He thought it best to leave her, so did.

Another month went by. Celeste and August met, unsatisfactorily. But there was always more time – the vessel had been launched three generations ago, and it was not even halfway to its destination. Space was very big; they learnt that every day. The youngest person on board would not live to see their arrival, not unless they lived to be the oldest person ever. This meant that Celeste and August, like all their generation, knew themselves to be merely in-betweeners – caretakers. Heartening messages from Earth, sometimes directed to them individually, tried to persuade them of their importance. *Without you . . .* Control was always positive.

Using opposite-speak, Celeste would say to August, 'I found Control's words very helpful. I now realize that my life will be deeply satisfying.'

'Yes,' he replied. 'Although my outlook is generally more positive than yours, I still find that a message from home gives me a real fillip.'

*Fillip* was such a stupid word. But not as stupid as *glory, honour, morale* or *freedom*.

Unobserved, at least so far as they knew, Celeste and August made their way to the washrooms adjoining the tennis courts. The showers, like the courts, had not been used for several decades – but a quick visiting check the previous day by August had confirmed that they still worked. At the same time, Celeste had pretended to be randomly accessing points-of-view via *it*, and had made sure that no-one could look at what went on inside the shower cubicle. This privacy, at least, had been guaranteed by the designers of the vessel: no cameras or microphones operated in either showers or toilets.

They stood, facing one another, still fully clothed – but they knew they would have to undress. They hadn't been able to bring towels; that would have been evidence, and much too suspicious. Even so, they were taking a risk: *it* might alert someone to the unusual running of a shower on an unoccupied deck. But since this hadn't happened after August's test-visit, it seemed unlikely to happen now.

August was a little nervous about undressing. However, he was far more worried about the next thing he had to say. This was a new kind of describing, describing in the presence of sensuous particulars, and he hated the idea of getting it wrong.

'So, when we take this shower,' he began, 'it's important for us to remember certain things.'

Without warning, Celeste crossed her arms in front of her tummy and began to pull her top upwards. A moment later, her head disappeared into a ruck of fabric. August looked, but knew he had to concentrate and keep going. 'We must remember how, despite what this feels like – we must remember how many other factors were involved.' He looked at Celeste's tummy and her tummy-button, which was so wide that he could easily have fitted his thumb-tip inside it. The impulse to do so was strong, but he kept on speaking. How many years was it since he had seen Celeste without clothes? 'I mean other factors, apart from just gravity – and that isn't the same here, either.' Celeste's top was now above her head in a shapeless bundle. Her bra-straps were dull grey, from repeated washing, not from dirt, not her dirt. The second-generation women had raided the underwear stores for themselves, just as they'd raided the toy stores for their children. This was Celeste's only bra – to use until she outgrew it, which would be soon. Then she would have to exchange it, through her mother, for an equally tatty replacement. 'We can keep the heat down,' continued August, 'and we will, to remind us that except in tropical countries – nearer the equator – rain usually comes as a *cold shower*.' He had begun, without really thinking about it, to undo his trousers. As if completely unembarrassed, Celeste was unhooking her grey bra. 'But what we'll never get a sense of is the droplets of water not just *falling*, dropping, but involving themselves, over a long dis-tance, in a dance with the breeze, and the complicated air-currents around trees or buildings – although we are still, like last time, out on the hilltop, just sheltered beneath a strong oak tree, before we step out sideways into the rain.' August had memorized this passage, and, as his trousers reached his ankles, was pleased to note he had not, so far, deviated. That was when he looked across, whilst bending down, and saw that Celeste had untied the drawstring on her loose cotton bottoms and was letting them drop to the floor of the cubicle. August, all of a sudden, could see what he had only imagined, the two fleshy sides, their join beneath hair – and so close was he, the scent of her was also suddenly present to him. 'It's a mistake to think we're really going to have a very similar experience at all,' he said. 'I mean, to the real one.' Celeste, in all her smoothness and musky fragrance, was now completely naked while he still had his top on and his trousers not yet freed from his ankles. He put his hand out to steady himself, and nearly touched her thigh.

'I know all that,' she said, seeming to speak from a completely different atmosphere – more practical, far more focused.

The trousers came free without him losing his balance. He stood up, relieved, and as he did so his fingertips brushed past her ribs. 'Sorry,' he said, then realized that was the absolute worst thing to say, particularly in the middle of a describing.

'Come on,' said Celeste. 'I'm getting cold.'

August could see the hairs starting to stand up on her golden-brown arms – hairs that were golden themselves. He felt leaden with blood. His cock was starting to get hard. There was nothing he could do about it, no image-obstacle he could create. Quickly, he ripped the T-shirt off over his head and dropped it down to crotch level. Celeste didn't seem to have noticed. August pushed open the glass of the cubicle door, and dumped his clothes outside with his shoes. Celeste did the same, carelessly tossing her sweatshirt and bottom on top of his. Their arms touched, and their legs did, too. How could she not be aware of this? His erection was full now, and as he stood up, it was pointing towards Celeste's cunt – as if halfway to finding its way there. Celeste's eyes dropped, and she saw it, but she said nothing; she didn't even make a joke. The shower controls were on her side of the cubicle, and to operate them she had to turn round. (*She saw it*, thought August.) It was the sight of Celeste's back that completely undid August. An arrow of golden hair fell gracefully from between her shoulders down to her buttocks. August felt a throb go through him, head to toe – although the top half of his head seemed to be missing entirely, and his toes had begun to tingle. The throb also travelled, at the same time, from the root of his cock to the tip; the same kind of jerk it often gave when he had just finished coming. August did not think he would come now, just as long as Celeste turned the cold water on. 'Ready?' she asked. August thought this might have been the withheld joke – and he almost laughed. Yes, he was completely ready. 'Yes,' he said. There were objects in his throat that hadn't been there a few moments before; not just a lump, more a family of mini-lumps, all fighting to be the one on top. 'Actually,' said Celeste, 'no. You're doing the describing, you should be the one in control.' August felt the cubicle darken, and it was as if his blood had darkened, too. He was now both leaden and airborne. Celeste turned round, then edged along the back of the cubicle, making room for August. Slightly crouched, he got to the controls in a couple of steps. His cock – a wise head – nodded in response to the movement. 'You're not saying very much,' Celeste said. This must have been a provocation. August couldn't reply, except to say, 'I can't.' The lumps had now multiplied to the extent that they made this almost literally true. 'Turn it on,' said Celeste. 'Turn on the rain.' She had closed her eyes, in expectation; she was standing there, entirely sensually receptive, hands by her sides. It wasn't a sexual pose, however. Instead, it was matter of fact, a little scientific and strict. It was a pure expression of Celeste. And because it was *this*, not just a difference of nakedness, August felt himself reach the very point. And then everything in the cubicle became more extreme; he felt as though his blood filled the sharp-edged space of it, as a solid, not a liquid — he felt as if his blood-heavy cock no longer merely existed in time but was the cause and issue of time: the thing dragging it, beat by beat, in whichever direction it was going. His hand turned the shower control, and the freezing water began to fall on them, washing away the cream of his come in an instant — before, he thought, she'd had any chance to see it.

And so Celeste began with, 'The snowflakes are coming down in long, slowly undulating lines — following the trajectory of the tresses of an old and beautiful woman's white and long and gone-slightly-crinkly hair; some flakes twist and corkscrew fairly regularly, others just waver a little — now and again — away from true: a slender hint of a bend here, a jink of a kink there. The woman, though, is a giantess, and her hair is the finest substance in all existence. She looks down upon the world, as if it were a baby in a cot, as if she were contemplating its likely life and grieving in advance for its death. Each snowflake, when it lands, lands silently – there is no sound even in the thickest flurry; the only change in acoustic is an increase in muffledness. That's the best way I can say it. Things go quieter. There are no longer any sharp edges for echoes to hone themselves on, for cracks and splinterings to sharpen. It is very satisfying to look at, especially from way up here where the view is so far and wide – down the hillsides and into the deep valleys of villages and small churches. New snow is the brightest white, and it makes the world it lands upon temporarily uniform in pallor. This is often interpreted, by writers, as a return to innocence – especially since young children take such delight in snow and are so closely associated with it. The landscape without snow must therefore be, working back from this, in some way guilty. A common thing for poets to say, particularly Romantic poets, is about the pure white covering over the dirt of industry, of factories and mills, giving a vision of how a workless world might be. But with the inevitable thaw of Springtime – unless the snow is the first beginning of an Ice Age – the grime and soot and dirt shows through again. The melt causes paths to become deeply muddy, which is unpleasant. The children cease their Winter games. They play with kites, instead, or stay indoors. We are not in Russia, but if we were this first cracking of the Winter ice would be a very dramatic, almost cataclysmic, moment. Here, in England, the snow just slowly starts to melt – drip-drip-drip, and the mud forms from the unfrozen earth mixed with the new water. This is the price to be paid: a vision of cleanliness followed by an increase in dirt. The weather, as we know, is always balanced, in what it gives and takes away.' August did not want her to finish. And she did have something else to say: 'Snow is welcomed by those citizens without the pressing need to work or travel. As long as their houses are tolerably warm, people take great delight in accompanying children out on to the hills to play. They slide downwards on sleighs – ice and snow being far more free of friction than grass. For the very poor, in England, snow is a miserable thing – although a snowy sky, with clouds white and thick, can be much warmer than a frosty and cloudless one without snow. Snowfall can actually increase mean ground temperature.' For a few calm moments, she said nothing. Then she said, 'Snow is a thing of air, even when it has settled.' And then, 'Unless the temperature of the earth is zero centigrade or below, the snow will not settle.' After this, she said nothing – and he said nothing, too.

But another voice spoke up, from the darkness over by the door. 'Why aren't there any birds?' They knew immediately who it was: Celeste's little brother, Hubble. 'I heard you,' he said, 'but why aren't there any birds?' It could only be Celeste's brother, because birds were his animal-obsession – and had been ever since he discovered emperor penguins, aged two. He was now twelve.

'Did you follow us?' asked Celeste, standing up. Her voice was completely different to before. It sounded terrifyingly maternal.

'No.'

'Then why are you here?'

'I found you.'

'No, you didn't. You followed us.' She was now confronting Hubble, who was only a couple of centimetres shorter than her. August went across.

'I just knew where you were. I *didn't* follow you this time. It was before – another time, last week. I followed you down here. So when you weren't around anywhere else, I knew you'd come here. I can help you with birds. Weather is okay but with birds it would be better. More realistic.'

'What would be better?'

'Your world.'

'What world?'

'The place you're talking about.'

'Hubble, you know nothing – and if you ever follow us again, I will kill you. I don't just mean I will do something nasty to you. I mean, I will strangle you to death when you're sleeping.'

In the dark, it was impossible to tell how Hubble was reacting to this threat; his face could not be seen, only the outline of his head.

'I am serious,' said Celeste, sounding it. 'I will kill you.'

Hubble said, 'But there would be birds. Where you're describing, there would be birds.'

Celeste now grabbed him. 'What do you know about describing?'

'I – you know.'

'You've been listening back?'

'I wanted to know.'

A quick check by August revealed Hubble's

search-paths. He had accessed, via *it*, audio of three of their describings. Only the first had he listened to the whole way through. That had been August's halting attempt at midnight frost. Ever since the day of the together-shower, the season had changed from Autumn to Winter. This had happened by mutual agreement, though nothing had been said. Cold weather was now their collaborative obsession.

'Okay,' said Celeste. 'Now you've been blocked. And now you leave us alone, and you don't tell anyone about it. Have you told anyone?'

'No.' Hubble sounded younger than he was.

'Remember, I will strangle you.'

'I didn't *tell* anyone. I just want to play, too.'

'It isn't a game,' said August. So far, he had left Celeste to deal with her brother. But if he said nothing at all, she might think him weak or indifferent. He wanted to add his threat to hers, by presence rather than words. *Killing* was extreme vocabulary, and could get them into trouble. August tried to be a little friendly: 'It is a private conversation, and we're blocking you out of it.'

'You'll have to explain,' said Hubble.

This was true. But older siblings blocked their younger brothers and sisters all the time – and the parents tended to insert a reciprocal block on the younger children's behalf, just so they felt equally protected from spying. With Hubble, there had never been a need before: he was far more interested in having *it* educate him about parrots, ostriches, dodos and lyre-birds. But now his obsession had coincided dangerously with theirs. He felt he might fulfil a lack. And now he knew of the existence of their world, the absence of birds in it was going to irk him, biologically. Hubble was never more irksome than when irked, especially biologically.

'Go,' said Celeste. 'And remember what I said. I did say it.'

August watched as Hubble's silhouette went out through the dim rectangle of the door. His footsteps sounded big-echoey as he passed the shower cubicles, and then he was definitely gone. Celeste immediately began to opposite-speak, although she knew it was unlikely her parents wouldn't get what she really meant.

'Maybe I shouldn't have been like that. It's not bad that Hubble knows. Perhaps we should let us join him.'

August understood what she was trying to say. This had been a trick of theirs for a number of years. It had started when Celeste said, 'I hate Australia. He's such a creep.' They must have been around ten. Australia had just been trying to explain something to them about the news, probably about Jerusalem. Celeste's language, in the presence of *it*, was a thrilling horror. *Creep.* He hadn't heard that before. None of the grown-ups spoke like that. *Creep.* She must have been researching slang dictionaries. But as soon as August heard the noun, and extrapolated it from the verb, he knew that's what Australia was, because that's what he did.

Of course, they were policed – their vocabulary was monitored by *it*. Violations were reported, either immediately or, more usually, at the end of the day; the parents got a brief report (along with basic biometrics, nutrition summaries, etc.), then they decided if they wanted to do anything.

After the afternoon on which she said *Creep*, August hadn't seen Celeste for three days. Her father – the Vice-Captain – had reviewed the footage, and was pretending to be very angry, although everyone found Australia annoying.

When the two cousins finally met again, Celeste immediately said to August that she had changed her mind. 'I'm so glad my parents grounded me. The last few days have been a true learning experience – an opportunity, really, rather than a punishment. Australia is a very nice, intelligent young man. I like him a lot. I think that he is a real asset to Mission.'

August looked into the centre of Celeste's pupils, and saw the question there: *Do you understand?*

He did.

'Oh, yes,' he said. 'Australia is my hero.'

From that time onwards, they used opposite-talk whenever they wanted to be negative – which was often. 'Vessel is such a beautiful ship.' 'I feel it's a huge privilege to be serving humanity in this way.' 'Wouldn't it be great if one of us became Captain?' Although *it* was very sophisticated, linguistically, sarcasm was beyond or beneath it – particularly as the way in which Celeste and August spoke when opposite-speaking was exactly how most of the crew-members spoke most of the time. The crew-members, however, were entirely sincere in their bland positivity; they knew no other tone.

And so, now, when Celeste suggested that they ask Hubble to join their describings, August knew she meant they must do all they could to keep him away and keep away from him.

'I agree,' he replied. 'He could really add to our knowledge.'

Celeste reached across and squeezed August's hand. It was spontaneous and affectionate; too much, almost, for him to bear.

'I regret threatening him. I hope he'll accept my apology.' This was for the benefit of Celeste's parents, who, as it turned out, grounded her for a week.

'*Kill* is not a word we use,' said her father. '*Kill* is not a concept we tolerate.'

'Sometimes,' said her mother, 'I don't understand you at all. Where did you come from?'

And this despite Celeste's having staged a reconciliation scene with Hubble as soon as she got back to their family's apartment.

'I'm sorry,' she said. 'I was just angry because I felt threatened by the knowledge of birdlife which you have and I don't. I really didn't mean it, you know.'

Hubble remained silent. He was sure, if of nothing else, that his sister had meant it. Celeste's passion was the most passionate on board. He needed it on his side, if he wanted to stay safe. Even more so if his time was spent in taxonomical study. After this, his nightmares became extremely elaborate, despite the best coaxing attentions of the psychologist. A vulture usually featured – either a Black vulture (*Coragyps atratus*) or a Lappet-faced vulture (*Torgos tracheliotus*).

They could not risk another trip down to the tennis courts – it was too dangerous. Hubble wasn't the problem; they could always check where he was, and be alerted if he approached. But too many questions had been asked already. Their parents had watched a little of the footage (listened, really, because it was so dark); not a vast amount, though – enough to call what they had been up to a *silly game*. Both Celeste and August were insulted by this, but they didn't say anything: they couldn't say anything. For *game*, although patronizing, kept them safe. At fifteen, they were still perceived as children. No-one had noticed the time-period they were absent in the shower, and *it* hadn't brought it to anyone's attention.

August's father, characteristically, had tried to be positive about the whole thing, awkwardly. He said, 'Son, I'm impressed with the meteorological knowledge you seem to have amassed. Why didn't you tell us?' August couldn't say, *Because it is against you – because everything I know is an escape as far away as possible from the place you have forced me to be.*

Celeste's father – taking a different approach to his brother – treated the whole thing as a joke, which suggested he was slightly more uneasy about this situation-arising than anyone else.

After a few weeks, Celeste and August felt able to meet again, in public. Through subtle opposite-talk, they agreed to wait until people's attention was elsewhere. (So little happened on board that the use of the word *kill* between two children was enough to bring common attention to bear. Celeste and August were watched, with eyes and through *it*.)

August assumed that their weather-planet would face a long pause. But then, one evening in the mess hall, Celeste surprised him by leaning close and whispering in his ear, 'High, white clouds bringing hail over the black horizon.' It was a whole describing, condensed into a single sentence. No-one seemed to have noticed, and the image transported August so completely that he found himself unable to eat. Instead, he hurried back to his bedroom and lay there, watching as the white clouds scudded towards him across a grey sky. When the hail fell, it battered him quite badly – he made the hailstones as big as his thumbs, and they hit him hard and everywhere. He suffered extensive bruising.

Almost as soon as the storm had passed, August began thinking of how he could possibly respond to such pure beauty. It would be quite wrong to rush: Celeste, he knew, was not expecting an immediate reply. Her mini-describe had obviously taken her a number of days to construct. He would do well to take the same time – and then choose, very carefully, the moment to deliver. Her describe had been as close to perfect as he could imagine. He must make his at least extremely different; but fit to follow, also.

For several days, he went over and over variations of frost – on treetops (oaks, of course), on grass-stems, on window-panes. He wanted to make his Winter as cold as possible, to indicate accurately. It was important she know. Snow, in itself, wasn't enough – wouldn't be enough. What he eventually decided upon, and whispered in her ear as they bumped, non-accidentally, in a typical corridor, was 'The deep lake is frozen solid.'

Celeste was clearly not as pessimistic as he, for

she spoke again the following morning. What amazed August this time was that she didn't bother to lower her voice. Across the long table at breakfast, she simply said, 'Sleet.' When someone asked her what she had said, she said, 'Sleep. I asked, *Did you sleep?*'

August was moved by the minimalistic approach. Again, *Frost* would have been his chosen word, his watchword, but it still wasn't cold enough. *Sleet* had brought with it so much atmosphere of long, average misery. Of all the weathers he had researched, *Sleet* was the most detested: neither rain nor snow; no use for anything but making children stay indoors, feeling frustrated. *Sleet* had been absolutely correct, for Celeste. He must find his own truth.

Yet even as he delivered it, he was unhappy with what he had to say: 'Freezing fog'. But Celeste touched his hand and said, 'Yes – thank you.' Perhaps she appreciated his insistence upon bleakness rather than unpleasantness.

Their minimal conversation continued, through her 'Drifts all up the steep hillside' and his 'Black ice', her 'Hoar frost' and his 'Snow falling on settled snow'. Then she decided it was time for Winter to end. 'Melt,' she said; 'Not a breath of wind,' he replied, trying to deflect her back towards January but also to remain ambiguous. She insisted, however, with 'Thaw', so he had to refuse: 'Re-freeze'. More tentatively, respecting his feelings, she offered 'Pale golden sunshine', the beauty of which brought him, only a few moments later, to 'reflecting on the frozen lake'. He was determinedly sub-zero. 'Tinkling; Icicles. The wind moves from North to North-West, then yet fur-

ther around; There are no clouds – the sky is ice-blue.'
Finally, Celeste ended Winter abruptly, absolutely.
'Heatwave,' she said, and stared at him until he broke
away. August sulked for two days, then capitulated,
'Rivers of melt,' he said, 'Rivers where there are no
rivers.' Celeste: 'The hill is bright green'; August: 'Men
and women swim in the lake.'

   Still, though, they were mostly separated. Missing
Celeste, August missed all the more what he had come
vaguely to call *life* or *real life*. He returned again and
again to the unfairness, to the cosmic injustice of their
situation, of his situation. He went to the observation
deck and looked out, not forward at the stars but back
across the lumpen curve of Vessel. August found it
humiliating even to think of himself as being trapped
on board such a piece of technological shit. (*Shit*,
another wonderful Celestine addition to his vocabulary.) Like brave young men throughout history,
he felt a strong calling – although, as yet, he had no
clear sense of what that calling might be. He still
yearned for greatness but had realized, instinctively
before rationally, that the life he had been born into
mitigated against glory in every single detail. His life
wasn't *life* – instead of *life* he had Mission; instead of *life*
he had distance travelled over time taken equals velocity; instead of the true heroism of danger and decision,
he had the corporate pride of a job well done. After all,
they were travelling on behalf of the whole human
race. And this crew had started out proportionally rep-
resenting – within the limits of feasibility – all the
nations, races, religions and non-religious creeds of
planet Earth. But as the first generation gave birth to

the second, and the second selected good genetic constituents for the third, and the third repeated the process, an inevitable homogenization started to take place. This wasn't yet revealed by everyone looking exactly the same, just by no-one looking all *that* different: the blackest skins had lightened and the blondest hair reddened. The process would continue: mothers of mulatto or quadroon extraction could select, from the gene-bank, to splice their partner's characteristics with those of pallidly Nordic or blackly African men, but their children would never be anything other than mixed. August, as far as *it* was able to inform him, was a quarter Polish, a quarter English (already mongrel), a quarter Australian aboriginal, four sixteenths Polynesian, Irish, Nigerian and Dutch. Celeste's genetic background varied only in the most minor details. Through their identical-twin mothers and brother-fathers, they had come to share many of the same physical characteristics: curly brown hair, broad nostrils, lush lips, sparkly green eyes, golden skin, and very long, loose limbs – all of which added up to an extreme, almost intimidating beauty. No-one else carried off being-from-everywhere-simultaneously/being-from-nowhere-ultimately anything like as well; some of them, if one were honest, looked a pug-faced, acne-skinned mess. Celeste and August were the golden children. Their attractiveness was a byword but also a serious problem, on board. For who would love such perfection? Who would step forward to try to win it? They seemed, at times, almost a different species – as if all the miscegenation of the rest of the crew had finally, miraculously, *simultaneously* worked. Celeste and August were, it appeared, the culmination – though no-one had consciously been working upwards. What was possible, after them, but an obvious degeneration? Yet there had to be an after, of course; Mission and love demanded it equally. And so Celeste and August became an irritation. To the men, Celeste was a moralizing temptation; to the women, August was a casually strolling one-man utopia – if they had been with him, the entire universe would have been a better place (and not just for them, for everyone; the love would radiate). The two cousins had talked over their predicament. 'I know I'm beautiful,' Celeste had said, initiating the topic, 'and you know you're gorgeous. By any standards. We've seen what people are like, on Earth – the actors, the models. We get the fan-mails. But the way we look means nothing. What good does it do us? Who are we going to attract?' The obvious answer, *We are going to attract one another*, could not be spoken. 'We're –' She lost the will to continue. August knew that Celeste knew he agreed with her, before she even spoke. Why didn't they just gaze at one another in sympathetic despair? For August, Celeste's eyes were the most fascinating objects in existence. They were different, each from each, the right eye seeming to be public, confident, rational, humorous and very Celeste; the left, however, was inward-looking and – however directly their gazes met – seemed to be turning constantly away. For Celeste, although August did not know it, it was the symmetry of his features that astounded, and attracted, her: she could find no single imbalance to them, and this made them seem an

43

argument *for* something – something utopian, perhaps, as the other women thought. This was Celeste's approach to *life*: nothing total; a matter of day-to-day survival, merely.

Celeste's little brother, Hubble, came up to her and said, 'I've been searching very hard, and I've found lots of different things which sound like lots of different birds. For example, when I put my thumbs together like this –' He cupped his small palms as if holding a tennis ball, then blew down into the slit between his thumbs. Celeste heard a high and vaguely ridiculous hooting-tooting, not dissimilar to the tone of her brother's speaking voice. 'That's a tawny owl, *Strix aluco*, native to the United Kingdom. And if you'll come with me to this one elevator down to Deck-3, it makes a squeak for half a second just like a blackbird's song. A blackbird is *Turdus merula*. It's also native to where you want. Then there is the left front wheel on one of the kitchen trolleys, which I've marked with string so I can identify it again. When it squeaks, it sings like a sky lark – *Alauda arvensis* – as long as you don't push it too fast or lean on it too heavily. I've experimented. And there are lots of other birds all over the place if you just listen – in the waterpipes and centrifuges, there are bitterns there, and when babies cry at night and –'

'*No*,' said Celeste, reasserting even with her first statement. 'You have been wasting your time, Hubba-Bubba. No-one is interested in your silly birds.'

She turned and walked away, and didn't listen to his protests, or his wail of upset. The use of his nickname

*Hubba-Bubba* was intended to let him know she still loved him, and so make her rejection more total. It hurt her to hurt him, but it was necessary; he was too dangerous. Either he didn't understand or he understood only too well. Whichever, they couldn't risk it. The described world was for her and August alone.

Approaching the door to his family's apartment, August heard loud weeping. He went close enough to confirm that, yes, that high-pitched ululation was definitely his mother's – then he turned and walked quickly away. (If he had run, *it* might have found this notable, and included footage in the end-of-day round-up. August didn't want his mother knowing he had avoided giving her comfort.) As so very little ever happened on board, apart from natural deaths, August knew that the weeping almost certainly meant bad news from Earth. Though as usual he had been doing his best to avoid hearing it, he knew, at least, that most of the recent news from Earth had been bad – news, he thought, could be defined as useless information about bad things which had already happened and so couldn't be helped. But the fact that there still *was* news at all was enough to prove the news wasn't as bad as it could be – as bad as a few people, his father among them, sometimes expected it to be.

'You heard?' said Aurelie, who was the first person he came across on his line of flight.

'Yes,' August replied, although he had deliberately not checked.

Aurelie, fine-boned and sensitive, was two years younger than August, and rarely spoke to him directly.

If he had bothered to think about it at all, he would have realized she was slyly sweet on him.

'It's terrible, isn't it?'

Aurelie was crying, too – as distressed as he had ever seen her. This made him wish he knew exactly what had happened, but he couldn't reveal his ignorance now.

'I'm sorry you're so upset,' he said, and moved to hug her. She accepted his embrace; it would be a special memory of hers until the day, quite distant, she died.

The next person he encountered was Australia's mother, Yvette. She was going to hug him whether he liked it or not.

'Just imagine their mothers,' she said. 'Try to imagine what they must be feeling.'

'It's terrible,' said August, hoping this – being what Aurelie had started with – would cover all possibilities.

'It is,' said Yvette. 'It's terrible beyond terrible – as if nothing had ever been terrible before.'

August extricated himself from her, thinking he should ask *it* to fill him in. But once away, he became superstitious: What if this terror really *was* something which would affect him, and would do so as deeply as it had Aurelie? Yvette, he dismissed; she was famously trivial, and would cry at less-than-nothings. He needed to see Celeste.

She was, *it* said, in her family's apartment. Aware of his where-search, she met him outside the door. He thought she looked pleased to see him – more *that* than anything else. And she knew the nature of the news; her parents would have told her.

'Let's go to the labs,' she said. 'I've made a discovery.'

Because he had been scrupulously paying no attention to Celeste, apart from their accidental meetings, he didn't know what she meant. What she meant was this:

A few days earlier, she had been strolling, bored, near the Deck-12 laboratories, when she smelled a smell more disgusting than any before. Sniffing up and down the corridor she went, until she found the door close to which the stench was strongest. She stood there for quite a while, trying to work out what it reminded her of – but nothing in her memory came close. It smelled *wrong* was what it smelled; it smelled like a bad mistake that could have serious long-term consequences for all those involved.

She knocked on the door, and a voice she recognized (there were no voices she didn't recognize) said, 'Come.'

It was Vladimir, the Chemist.

Inside the lab, the smell was ten times as strong. She covered her mouth and felt the gag-reflex start in the walls of her throat; this brought back body-memories of choking on breastmilk as an infant.

'I'm sorry,' said Vladimir. 'It is a little strong, isn't it? I didn't realize quite how strong it was going to be. What do you think?'

'It's disgusting,' Celeste said. 'What is it?'

'Good,' Vladimir said, replying only to her *disgusting*. 'What else is it?'

She was disappointed; when she'd come through the door, and he'd apologized, she'd thought there was a chance he would treat her as an adult – this was more like taking part in one of his silly experiments for a little improvement in virtù, and nothing to spend it on anyway.

'It makes me feel like being sick,' she said. 'So tell me what it is. Am I going to get horribly ill and die?'

'Do you think I'd be standing here so calmly?' Vladimir asked.

She turned to leave. If he wasn't going to answer ... However, he understood – or began to behave as if he did. His voice, softer but more scientific, said, 'It's 1,4-diaminobutane – chemical formula $C_4H_{12}N_2$. Interested?'

Blank, she looked; completely blank; deliberately.

'Also known as putrescine, as in putrid, putrescence.'

'Meaning?'

'Rotting.'

'Meaning?'

Celeste had never seen any point in science before – not unless it helped her describe. Science was what had shot them into space, stuck them inside the hell of Vessel.

'It's an earth smell,' Vladimir said, not unaware of the contents of Celeste and August's notorious private conversations. 'Tell me, what do you think smelled like this?'

Hooked, she turned and returned to his side. 'I don't know – like something I never want to smell again.'

'Yet you came in to investigate. Interesting.'

'It was disgusting, and I wanted to know what it was.'

48

'A perfectly normal reaction. All right, I'll tell you about it.' Celeste hated the way born teachers talked. Vladimir was looking for an apprentice, and she knew it. 'I've been synthesizing a few earth-chemicals, just for fun – particularly those with interesting smells. If you look in that rack over there, you can see what I've been up to. Only very small quantities.'

She went across to the stoppered test-tubes Vladimir had indicated. All the labels were written in chemical symbols – $C_2H_4O_2$, $C_{10}H_8O$, $C_{10}H_{14}O$ – so they told her nothing; apart from the fact that carbon, hydrogen and oxygen, which she remembered only too well from his classes, were involved.

'You can open any of them,' Vladimir said. 'I haven't made anything properly dangerous – *it* doesn't allow me to.'

She reached for the clear liquid on the extreme right, then pulled her hand back. 'So, these smells are like Earth smells?' she said.

'They're rough chemical approximations, from what *it* tells me. But they're the closest thing we're going to get, out here.'

His casual words made Celeste feel, once more, their hopeless isolation. They weren't *out here*, they were *out nowhere, beyond nowhere*.

'I want to fetch my cousin. I don't want to smell them without him.'

'Very loyal, I'm sure. But, anyway, I'm about to finish for the day. If you're still interested, and haven't forgotten about it completely, why don't you both come tomorrow? Any time is good for me. I'm always here. I have no other life.'

Vladimir was married to a woman called Atima; they had a son called Seaborg. Celeste did not consider his words strange – she did not consider them at all.

'We will come,' she said, and tapped the test-tubes one by one on the stoppers. 'Maybe not tomorrow. Some other time.'

'Okay,' said Vladimir, who had a thick brown beard and was disguised-handsome underneath.

She made it to the door, before her curiosity returned. 'Putrescine,' she said.

'That's right,' Vladimir replied.

'And so what *does* it smell of?'

'Death,' said Vladimir. 'It smells of dead things and of death.'

As she entered the corridor, Celeste's face broke open, and she smiled more broadly than she had in years. What a gift for August, when she was able to see him again!

And now the bad news from Earth had given Celeste a chance to take August down to the labs, and show him what she'd found. *Show* despite it being smells. But when they got there, the door was locked. A check with *it* told them that Vladimir was in his apartment. Everyone wanted to be with those they were closest to. Vladimir was with Seaborg.

Celeste was disappointed. She inhaled softly, but nothing of the smell of death was left. 'I'll tell you anyway,' she said. 'Let's walk.'

She began; August understood immediately.

'Just imagine it,' Celeste said. 'He could do anything. He could make special scents, just for us.'

'Rain,' August said. 'That's what I want to smell most of all – rain from the very top of the hill. Do you think he can synthesize that?'

'I don't know. Everything's chemical to begin with. Rain is just water falling from the sky.'

'But it must smell of something. Doesn't it smell of clouds? Doesn't that make it smell different to just being in a pool on the ground? The sea smells, I know that. It smells of salt but of much more than salt.'

'They talk about earth – earth, mud, the ground itself, not the planet.' *They*, they both knew, were the poets. 'They talk about how that smells when it's rained on. I think rain is a combination of cloud-smelling water and smells from earthy things getting wet. Your hair, when it's wet, smells different from when it's dry.'

August wasn't sure at first whether this was an allusion to their rain-shower. If, by the word *your*, she meant *him*, then she also must mean to remind him of the only time when she could have smelled his hair, wet. And why would she be doing that? Either to arouse or embarrass him. Or, also, though less likely, to torture. But *your* in that sentence could mean her, or everyone. In fact, Celeste was so thoroughly thinking of that melancholy smell that she wasn't being careful about phrasing. Her speech was in-accurate rhapsody around the idea of close-to-Earth experience.

They spent some time discussing the different smells of hair, and whether it smelled at all like grass – and then they moved on to the question of snow, which must smell different to rain as being water in a different state.

'Perhaps Vladimir will know,' August said. 'Or perhaps he will be able to find out from *it*.'

'But we don't ask *it*,' she said. 'That's the whole point. We make up our world from our heads, and from what we can read.'

'This would be objective,' he said. 'Like the shower. We might learn something important.'

Celeste disagreed, but felt wonderful to be with August again. People would be preoccupied with the bad news for several days; they were free.

She allowed herself to nudge into him, as they strolled along. He did not fail to notice the hidden touch accomplished by this; it remained as an area of felt-tingling all up his left arm. In reply, he tenderly refrained from making an equal and opposite nudge; leaving her the dignity of the accidental. All the same, she felt him where he would have been – where she knew he wanted to be. The two cousins, for this moment, were terribly happy.

Celeste had *it* alert her when Vladimir returned to the lab. Then she told August to meet her there. It was three days after the very bad news. Vladimir, opening the door, seemed a much older man; new silver in his beard.

The two of them were impatient, and found it very difficult not to ask him immediately whether he had the smell of rain.

Vladimir began with putrescine, wanting to gauge August's reaction, as well. The chemical could be dangerous if inhaled in large quantities, so Vladimir only allowed him a whiff.

Although Celeste had told August a little about it, he was still unprepared for a smell that seemed so aggressive, so unnecessarily nasty, so anti-life.

'It's the smell of death,' said August.

'Yes, you are right – exactly right,' Vladimir said. He turned to Celeste. 'Did you tell him?'

'No,' she said, which was true. She had just said it was of Earth and that it was exciting. To tell August any more would be to destroy the surprise. And she had wanted to see him discover the death part for himself. (She had been sure he would.)

'More accurately,' said Vladimir, turning back to August, 'it is the smell of death *after* death – the smell of dead things which have been left to rot. This is what the body of some kind of animal – a dog, for example – would smell like a few days after it died – if you just left it lying where it was, in the sun. It would start to decompose. You remember what a dog is?'

The question was for both of them.

'Of course,' said Celeste, annoyed.

August was thinking of the classic cartoons on which he had been brought up, and of their many dogs – of Pluto and Snoopy, of Goofy and the Hundred and One Dalmatians, of Muttley, Scooby-Doo, Jumpah, Spangle and Captain Superwoof. Of course, he knew that dogs were dogs and cartoons were cartoons, and therefore that cartoon dogs were only cartoon dogs. And yet the image now in his mind, mutated by the stench, was not of any of the dogs in nature films he'd watched, but of Snoopy – a decomposing Snoopy.

Cartoon characters didn't really have insides, though; Snoopy needed some cartoon ribs to poke out through his rotting cartoon skin. Although he tried to persuade his mind to present him with another image, August was unable to get dead-Snoopy out of his head. This putrescine smell was what Snoopy would smell like, four or five days after he died, if he was left out in the sun. But most cartoon characters never died – Snoopy never died, so this was an impossible smell. August's brain, it was clear, was doing everything it could to evade the reality of the fact – stinking – of death.

'Enough of that one,' said Vladimir. 'Try the next along.' He wasn't following a strict order, so this probably wasn't a real experiment. *it* was recording them, and he might watch the footage later for purposes of study.

'That's—' Celeste said, the note of her voice t-tooting slightly in the air-column of the test-tube. 'That's lemon,' she said. 'Like lemonade. It smells a bit like lemonade tastes, without the sweeteners.'

August gave it a quick sniff, but already he'd lost interest.

'And the next —' said Vladimir.

They couldn't identify it; it was a fruity smell: pears. Then came an easy one: roses.

The following was both pleasant and unpleasant. Pears and lemon had made them salivate slightly; this did, too, but not because it smelled edible or appetizing.

'It's woodsmoke,' Vladimir said, '$C_{10}H_{14}O$ – thymol.'

'A fire would smell like this,' said August, transported. He had smelled burnt-out circuits; they were charred plastics, melded metals. This smell was wonderful – so rich. There were stories inside it, of battles and expeditions.

They had three more to go. Apples, which they knew. Two more. Perhaps earth wasn't here, nor rain; rain on earth.

'Another fruit?' Celeste said, of the penultimate scent. 'No. Wait.'

She let August try it, briefly.

'I know that,' he said.

Celeste held the tube up to her high-arched nostrils and took another deep breath. 'Grass,' she said, the true answering coming from somewhere. 'That's – it's grass.'

'Yes!' said August.

'How did you know that?' asked Vladimir, shocked, almost disturbed. He hadn't searched their conversations thoroughly enough to discover this fascination. 'Most people would never have got it.'

Celeste turned to August and mouthed the word: 'Grasmere.'

'What's that?' Vladimir asked, now thoroughly confused.

'I knew,' Celeste said.

'Yes, but *how* did you know?'

Celeste did not want to say. But when she saw August waiting for her, then the question became his, as well as Vladimir's – and she felt obliged to answer.

'I knew because *that* is the smell of grass. I can't explain any more.'

'It's what they call a *green smell*,' said Vladimir. 'But trees are green – and moss, and melons, and lots of other things.'

'Do you have earth?' asked Celeste, very moved.

'No,' said Vladimir. 'No earth. What you have there is a weak solution of hexanal, $C_6H_{12}O$.'

Celeste walked away from them, into a corner – then she turned round and beckoned August. He went to her, and she held up the grass test-tube between them; they brought their faces close so they were together in the fresh, light, lawny smell. 'It's early May,' she whispered. 'A sunny morning. Not a cloud. An hour ago, there was a brief shower. It's a beautiful, beautiful day.' She spoke deep into his ear – close, breathy – and he, inhaling, had the illusion that the grass-smell was coming from inside her, that her lungs were its sweet source. He imagined green and waving strands within her, blown-this-way-that-way by the wind of respiration. He had always known (always since he became himself) – always known that if he turned her inside-out she would unfold around him to become the whole landscape of the Lake District; all of it was there, indwelling, known.

Her feelings were reciprocal, but not mirror; she felt, too, as if she were exhaling the smell and August were receiving it. She felt earth-like.

Vladimir looked on, unnerved by this strange intensity between the cousins. He had the feeling that he had supplied them with some new game. It was thrilling; he had expected them to be bored – they usually were, adolescents, when he spoke. These two seemed transported, as if he had ceased entirely to exist. 'It's a very fresh smell, isn't it?' he said. 'Very pleasant.' The cousins couldn't keep him out for ever; August could hear the sound of the chemist's voice, but did not understand the words it said. He opened his eyes, and let them come to rest on the scientist in his much-stained labcoat. 'Can we keep it?'

'No,' said Vladimir. 'I can't let any chemicals out of the lab.'

'But it's not dangerous,' Celeste said, instantly passionate. 'You said it's not dangerous.'

'Not particularly,' Vladimir said. 'But there can't be any exceptions.'

Celeste looked at him, smiled, then pulled August close to her and poured the grass-smell over their touching heads.

August was shocked but overjoyed – he knew instantly there would be negative consequences to issue from this act, but that he and she would suffer them together (and in suffering them together, they would be brought closer; that, he suspected, behind the moment's impulse, was why she had really done this). The thought of them smelling so extraordinary, and so extraordinarily the same, for days and days afterwards, was wonderful. He would never, he knew, have had the simple courage and defiance to do what she had done. His admiration for her made him want to kiss her, properly, for the first time; they couldn't be any closer, their lips were only not touching because breathing their grass-scent as well as inhaling it was so important to both of them; mouths as well as noses. So beautiful, she was – so beautiful and free in her actions. (Vladimir was shouting at them; August became aware of this.) August was in love with Celeste's actions; his greatest hope, though he felt he might never find out, was that she was performing them in order, *partly* at least, but sometimes even *mostly*, to impress him. In which case, the doings were less spontaneous and, he might suppose, if he'd had time to think of it, less admirable – but, coming from that motive, he would have regarded them as infinitely more lovely.

'What have you done?' shouted Vladimir, again.

'If you'd given it to us, we wouldn't have,' said Celeste.

'But it's stupid.'

'We wanted the smell.'

'You'll have to shower immediately. If it gets in your eyes –'

'It's in our eyes – it's in our eyes all the way from the front to the back. We see the smells. We see the earth. We see the grass. We don't just see transparent liquids. We're there, not here. You can't stop us – what you have of Earth is ours, not yours.'

Celeste took August's hand and began to walk towards the door.

As they passed the metal worksurface of the table-top, she carelessly dropped the test-tube upon it; it tinkled, did not break, rolled off and shattered on the floor.

'We have what we want, now,' she said.

August went with her into the corridor, ecstatically – so ecstatic that he almost left himself behind him. He couldn't think of anything to say. He wasn't present enough to do thinking. 'You –' That was as far as he got into the impossible sentence before her mouth was on his and they were now truly kissing.

Vladimir raised the alarm, and their fathers came to get them. When intercepted, Celeste and August were on their way up to the tennis courts. They were taken straight to the showers, where – separately, but within hearing distance – they were forced to wash the hexanal off their already reddening skins. Then, dressed in new clothes, they were brought to the bridge, where the Captain spoke to them with re-strained anger. He was a tall man, fifty-seven years old, bald but with a very long beard of glossy brown hair. His given name was Abd al-Salaam. When he addressed Celeste, he looked at her father; when he addressed August, he looked at Celeste. Their behaviour, he said, and repeated, was disgraceful. One day, they would be officers responsible for the running of affairs, and, one day, they would look back upon this day with shame. At it turned out, the Captain was entirely wrong; neither Celeste nor August would be promoted – and, when they looked back, it was with frustration.

Their punishment, which began immediately, was – as August had expected – worse than last time. They were grounded for a minimum of a month, given strictly limited and policed access to *it*, and required to attend daily sessions with the psychoanalyst, Mary: Celeste in the mornings, August in the afternoons.

When the Captain had finished speaking, he asked if they had anything to say.

August did not move his head.

'You are stupid,' said Celeste. 'All of you. That's why we're being punished – for not being stupid enough.'

Their parents took them home, and had things of their own to say. Then, at about the same time, Celeste and August were told to go to their rooms. Each of them knew that this was what the other would be doing – and each of them felt strengthened by this knowledge.

*I know you are thinking of me*, said Celeste, silently, as though August could hear.

*I am thinking of you*, said August, in his head.

Their psychoanalysis began the next day. And in this way, over the next few weeks, very indirectly, they were able to maintain contact – for vocabulary introduced by Celeste in her sessions would, eventually, inadvertently, be used by the analyst in her sessions with August. He heard these words almost as if Celeste had spoken them. The analyst, Mary, was not very intelligent, and kept returning to the exploration of dreams they had invented and motives they did not have. She could never resist the leading question. This was partly because her repeated viewings of the describing-footage had left her dangerously curious. No-one else on board was as interesting, she felt, or as needful of analysis, or as glamorous, as Celeste and August. (Mary was dull-eyed and plain.) The trouble was, neither of them would speak unless forced to – and psychoanalysts of Mary's ultra-Freudian sort weren't meant to force anyone to speak.

'Tell me more about hail,' Mary would say.

'I don't know very much about hail,' August would say.

'Look it up,' Celeste would reply.

'But I want to hear it in your words,' Mary would say.

'They're not my words. I just let them speak through me,' August would say.

'I'm sure you already have,' Celeste would reply. 'Heard it in my words.'

'There seems to be a certain defensiveness in your attitude,' Mary would say to August, and with Celeste *defensiveness* would be replaced by *defiance*. 'Perhaps we could explore that further.'

They explored nothing.

Celeste, alone, did a describe just for herself – although without speaking a word aloud. It was a different kind of describe.

'The best thing on board this whole ship are the irises of your eyes. No-one's messed with them – they look like precious fabric, green and black silk, all stretched out from the shining hole of the centre. I can't see into your pupil at all, although I know what's in there; the only thing I see in your pupil is a distorted version of my own horrible face. Or maybe not that distorted: I have big bug-eyes; I'm a big bug-eyed monster, because I want to look so hard at you. I want to stare my way into where you are, where you live somewhere inside you. My eyes want to become *your* eyes, not so that I can see me as you do but so that I can see you as you seeing you reflected in my eyes. Then something beautiful would happen, with a short circuit of that bottomless green. (I'm sounding like you, now.) Two circles times by two circles times by two circles, etcetera. Your eyes look like pale, stretched *it*-images of streaky moss. Their surface is what I imagine a raindrop's as being, falling through the night-sky – a glistening purity. Brighter than all the light going into them, your eyes are. I've only ever seen *it*-images of rich green moss – though there are one or two small patches of algae here and there on board. Nothing in the big weather is like them; the sky never goes a green like that. As pure as an empty I mean cloudless sky. But there is weather on the surface and weather behind your eyes. Yes, they are also like starbursts I have seen: streaky light outflung and sometimes obscured by clouds of dust. August, through all of the things they should have seen, and are denied, your eyes are still part of the earth. That is what was meant for them. All those visions are in them, despite their exile. Am I worth your looking at? How I long to be.'

August, also, did a private describe – so in sympathy were they; twinlike, though kept apart.

'You're not very like meteorologic – like anything meteorological. Colours, the sky is useless at. I can't compare you to a blue thing. Sometimes, when the sun is setting, especially on autumn clouds, I think it goes orange-red with a bit of pink; a sort of exaggeration of fleshtints. The whole sky would be seen glowing from behind, as you glow from within. (I hope that isn't because your sun is about to set.) But those colours would be completely wrong, for getting you right like I so want to. You are precious like a very small thing, a tiny frog, but also magnificent like the whole firmament.' He had been saving *firmament* up. Other words he was keeping were *cerulean, dappled, sepulchral* and *love*. 'Your curly hair is of course a cumulonimbus – *nimbus* not *cirrus*, although *cirrus* means *hair*. It piles up and up in a funny way. I want to cut it all off, just so I can have the pleasure of watching it grow again – coming out straight and then twisting when it gets damp. But I don't want to describe your hair. Instead, your skin – they way it rises and falls as it goes down your body, over ribs and hips, your skin is like slight alterations in barometric pressure during a month of set-fair weather. The quarter-circles on the cuticles of your nails are like the sun setting through a thick winter mist, all the gold gone white. When I listen to the blood in your veins, I hear water cascading down a rocky mountainside. Your blood can't be wild, it flows within courses – if it didn't, you would die. But it batters against the corners and edges it meets. The will of its gush is streamlike, in spate. Your breath is my sweet summer breeze – it doesn't seem to come from your blushing-brushing lung capillaries but reaches me across open hillsides covered with flowers I can't name and grass I'll still never touch, though I have nearly smelled it. I want to roam all across you, not like a miniature person on your surfaces but like a tiny ghost with access to every last little part of you – a tiny floating ghost who can control exactly where he wants to go. But I would also want to be my full-size self, at the same time. Then I could know you properly, from both scales at once. When we kissed – we would kiss – if I had what I wanted, we would kiss – at the same time we kissed I would be also in your heart, and would feel the excitement of its adrenalized acceleration all around me.'

The punishment went on and on. It was almost that time of year when their day-apart birthdays fell. But everybody recognized they could not be kept apart for ever – Vessel was too small for that. And after a couple of months people's attention began to waver; there was more bad news from Earth. Eventually, the cousins were able to arrange a meeting while everyone was asleep but the skeleton-crew on the command-deck.

Together.

An extreme and exquisite sweetness was all upon the air – carried up to the walled hilltop from some unknown source; scent of flowers and, more specifically, roses. How could *they* be near by? There was no garden, so high up, and they were not native, like gorse and pinks. Perhaps some disappointed lover had abandoned a bouquet, undelivered love-gift, rejected heart-offering – thrown it from the path as he approached the summit. Or perhaps the breezes, unnaturally strong, strongly unnatural, had themselves fashioned an air-garland from the faraway village blooms, and borne it hither; a thing never known before.

Also, reaching up through this soft and absurdly fragrant atmosphere, came the lipping-lapping sounds of a trickling stream. But, again, here was surely too high up for that – the becks began below the treeline, far out of earshot, although there was no-one present to hear; all was unpeopled landscape. Perhaps, though, an underground rivulet, tiny and just beginning, ran shyly away even from these exulted places. Splash it went, and splish, licking with a lush lisp under the mossy rock of this sky-nearest point.

As the first cloud moved, a caress of light slid all the way down the long, sweeping side of the peak. Dark followed this, then light, then again dark: the rhythm of the passing clouds was almost regular – and as the warm breath of the wind blew faster, so the rhythm of fade and flash accelerated. The air was tensile; the ground seemed earthquake-capable. And far below, the surface of the lake changed, moment by moment, from just-polished silver to tarnished and thumb-printed pewter.

Quicker went the clouds, almost as if time itself were speeding up. The sweep-past of dark became true flicker; white shapes glimpsed on one horizon reached the opposite in the time it would have taken to breathe but one shallow-fast breath. Then an even odder effect of the light became noticeable: the lake-valley was hidden by a deep shadow – a dark so absolute that any viewer could no longer have been sure the water was still there. And the hilltop, at the same time, was blessed with a glory that could only, and yet wrongly, have been described as blinding. It was hard not to believe that, in some miracle, the exposed altitude-stone would catch fire.

All at once, the ground began violently to shudder. This was impossible; in the geology of the Lakes, earthquake activity was unprecedented. But, still, pebbles began their cascando descents, areas of the drystone wall slumped into heaps, gorse bushes trembled as though they were deathbound beasts, and the waves upon the water formed into concentric circles. The very horizon seemed, if this were possible, endangered. From moment to moment, the tremor intensified – until, with an agony of strangeness, the hilltop split into a volcano, all fiery, all a-gush. And then, suddenly, the air above the landscape was filled with the panicked cries of a thousand different, inappropriate birds. They shrieked and screeched, as if they had flown over a fire and set their fine feathers alight. Where had this cacophony sprung from? Surely this arisen life hadn't just been hiding within the landscape, awaiting the eruption?

In an instant, the dark of the lake-valley dissipated. Yet, at the same time, the clouds above it became brown-clotted and flecked with black. Was this the so-called dawn-chorus? Had some freak of nature displaced it from its rightful sunrise hour? Birds were silly, easily confused. They had been known to sing, mistakenly, at powerful midnight light-sources. But these were not ordinary or natural or reasonable birds. For one thing, they sounded far louder and bigger than they should have done – almost the size of human beings. The very air seemed to quiver under the assault of their noise. And as the sound grew in volume and derangedness, the true explanation for this avian scream became both clearer and more annoying.

And then, just as suddenly as it had started, the insane shrieking ceased. It was as if all the birds had, simultaneously, taken flight – not away over the horizon but directly down into the earth; burying themselves in quiet.

After a while, during which the lake-blown breeze

blew loudly, voicing itself against the steep hillside, it seemed certain the birds – unnatural birds – had gone away, and were not going to come back.

What was perhaps most incredible about their intervention was that, from start to finish, not a single feather had been seen across the landscape. Yet their volume had been such that it was hard to believe they had all that time been beyond the horizon's rim. Even after they silenced, it was as if the whole world had been affected – affected to the point of upset. Lava from the hilltop had flowed down into the lake, leaving the landscape scarred, but there was now no sign at the peak that an eruption had ever taken place. The grass thereabouts had a disarrayed look, and the breezes overhead blew in all directions at once. The causal flow of the weather had been interrupted to an extent which, although not divine, was greater than the merely meteorological. The clouds began to move in ways which, although not quite random, were amazingly uncoordinated – they shredded, twisted, were thrown together, shrunk, crumbled to snow-showers. Then a new spirit began to express itself through them, an animalistic wildness. One large slow cumulus would attempt to make a stately progress from horizon to horizon, but halfway across would be attacked by a pack of smaller, wolf-like clouds. These dipped and zagged and swung and leapt in all directions – sometimes to do so splitting into four sub-clouds, quarter-wolves. On one occasion, an especially vicious puff of white accelerated straight through the belly of a bloated, trundling cumulus. Out the other side it shot, leaving the larger cloud – in a way that any viewer would have found quite absurd yet deeply touching – mortally wounded. Rain began to shoot sideways from the two thus-created holes; the cumulus fell towards the ground, tilting gradually until nosediving. It seemed likely that it would crumple away, then, in huge puffs of mist. Instead, it seemed to turn from a suspension of minuscule airborne water droplets into a cloud-shaped wave. And then the cloud-wave condensed even further, into an anvil of supersolid water. Never before had rain ever approached such mass. A second lake had materialized in the air; and begun to fall. The ground where it made its impact was as if bombstruck; trees splintered, boulders shattered, landscape-features which had lasted aeons found themselves instantly obliterated.

When the mist cleared, all that was left of one particularly picturesque hillock was a deep, overflowing crater. And the manner in which the mist cleared was this: by rising (bizarrely) as further packs of wolf-clouds which, in their turn, attacked the complacency of cumulus after crossing cumulus. Each of these, wounded, shearing off to the side, descended upon the landscape with the force of a million-tonne hammer. Dells and dales, fells and knolls were smithereened; atrocious damage was sustained to micro-ecosystems; the ground shook even more violently than during the earthquake. To any viewer, it would have seemed hard to believe the Lake District wouldn't be destroyed completely.

Once the sky was cleared of cumuli, further battles developed between wolf-clouds. These were even more fragmentary, and involved two or three of them banding together to attack a weaker, perhaps injured, third or fourth. Victims were ripped apart, water gushing from their insides – so much water that it was hard to believe they had been able to fly, let alone so dartingly. The sky became quite empty, with only one final duel between two maimed and leaking clouds remaining to be fought out. In this case, the loser plunged straight down into the lake and the winner, also mortally wounded, limped off over the hills towards the west.

The air was not yet finished, though, for it seemed as if the clouds had merely been the visible manifestations of clashes going on violently between updraughts, crosswinds, shears and mini-tornadoes. Now there were no watery obstacles, these aloft-battles became more violent. The few trees and low bushes that still remained were wrenched this way and that – branches yanked off and roots loosening their hold. Leaves were sucked up in twisters that formed, ran into one another, cancelled each other out or continued with redoubled force. When they became powerful enough, these vortices grabbed pebbles and stones from the ground and in seconds propelled them hundreds of metres into the air – from whence they tried to rain down on the ruined landscape, but instead further warring buffets whipped them crossways. The air was deadly thick with rapid projectiles – any bird trying to fly across now would be blasted to feathery bits. The surface of the lake was ripped to pieces, far worse than in the midst of the most violent hailstorm ever recorded – stones skipped across the choppy surface only to be sucked up once more into the high-dotted sky.

Then, from one moment to the next, the battle was won, and all the air began to move in a single direction – round and round above the centre of the lake. A huge, twisting hurricane was forming. As it grew and gained power, it began to suck water up out of the lake – a vast waterspout thousands of metres high. At the very top of this, almost beyond the troposphere, the water fountained and then began to fall down – not as dispersed rain, but in a kind of outer tube, surrounding completely the uprising column. By the time the jet had exhausted itself, it was as if the lake had purposely turned inside-out. A final few splashes disturbed the surface, and then all the landscape became absolutely still. The sky was windless – as if such a thing had never been known, and all the destruction had been purely Earth-caused.

And then a thick mist began to ascend from the flat, devastated grass – the moisture of the clouds arising once more, resurrected. Quite soon it was impossible to see from one side of the lake to the other, and, within moments of this, the whole thing had disappeared entirely behind a wall of completely opaque grey-white. Although the fury of the winds seemed quite spent, the atmosphere overall, contrary to what might have been expected, was not calm – there was stinging tension, as if each droplet of moisture in the air were grabbing its place only by suppressing all of those hopeless-helpless-hapless ones beneath it. Yet there was something unexpectedly sublime about the total invisibility of the landscape; it was lost to itself already. And then, quite shockingly, the whole planet was cleft in twain – a division that began up in the highest heavens, and proceeded rapidly down to the very epicentre; clouds, also; mist, also; severed down the middle, with terrible rending cries. The Lake District – the place where the line of separation most cruelly fell – was parted from itself: west from east, lake from mountain. Up in the sky, as the gap grew, the cause of this split became apparent: two moons and two suns, combining the complex forces of their gravities, pulling asunder. The moons appeared to burn red even as the suns glowed icy-pale. And, down below, as the lovely world was destroyed, all the superheated steam normally kept below the surface shot out in agonized screeches. Each half-globe's sound-grief was beyond volcanic. The two exposed circular cross-sections, now facing nothing but nothing, nothing but the emptiness of space-time, were a pair of huge, angry, almost-identical wounds. They wept molten rock, spilling it out like scalding tears of thwarted passion. Unbelievable heat came from inside each of them; enough to sear the moons and scorch the suns. The cleft down the middle of each was an ugly, brutal thing, not at all laser-done and neat; bisection of an integrated world cannot be clinical. Boulders which crossed the dividing line had to decide one way or the other – if not, they tumbled off into the rapidly widening gap of emptiness.

But the two halves of the world, the west and the east, would not be parted quite so easily; a sweet gravity made each half yearn towards the other for as long as they were in sight. Finally, however, the forces of separation proved overwhelmingly powerful.

As soon as they were parted, the two halves of the Lake District began to move in different seasons. The lake-half, attended to by moons, rapidly became a frozen, tundra-bitched world, and the sun-struck hill-half fell victim to a furious heat. The lake turned solid ice, top to bottom; the hill turned desert, all moisture from the lake's rains gone, topsoil blown away by lacerating winds. It was broken; all of it, the world, the mountain and the lake, all entirely split. And with this parting, an infinitesimally delicate and tender ecological balance existing only between them had been destroyed.

Over the next few weeks, the landscape surrounding the lake continued to throw off all heat – eventually approaching absolute zero. Strange protective-looking constructions of ice formed on what had been the water's margins. There were no colours but white and very pale blue. This half-world, windless, was almost without sound, but what deep shiftings and crackings there were echoed and re-echoed for a long time – every surface sent back soundwaves, largely undiminished; nothing the moon had to say was allowed to be absorbed. The sun came also, too close, and the heat from its white face was quite vicious. It came back and back and back – some change in the compass of its orbit must have taken place. But however close it approached, and however furiously it shone, the landscape never unfroze and the lake gave no crack of melt or softening.

For months, the lake lay beneath a thick horizontal wall of ice – keeping out everything; but there was something in there, deep beneath the unwet waters, something tiny but growing.

One day, a single timid bird was heard to twitter – seeming, as it did so, almost to apologize for its own existence. There was a whirl of ice, a tornado across the wastes of snow. The bird was not heard from again for several days. When it did return, however, it sang so beautifully that the ice seemed to listen, to reverberate in sympathy with the high, dipping notes. But the fury of the ice-devils, twisting and rapid, rose again. A third time the bird returned, and this time the half-landscape made no attempt to rid itself of the glory and simplicity of its needed song. The tiny bird rested by the lakeside, sending forth dry notes, hot chirrups. It sang of a desert waste – a desert not of ice but of sand; an empty expanse, waterless, bereft of organic life. Then, when the bird flew off, it travelled across space, going from one half-planet to the other. The sand-desert, it had been visiting for quite some time already. Here, its tone was rising, insistent. Amid the dusty, recalcitrant barrenness, the bird seemed to offer hope of change. And as it returned from its first three visits to the lake-half, the birdsong became increasingly exultant. Perhaps the whirlwinds blew a little more gently, in the aftermath. Certainly, the bird was able to sit in a pocket of calm whilst it delivered its message. Then it would be gone, for hours though not days – and it would return, slightly altered in tone; more certain of its mission. Back and forth it bravely flew, traversing the emptiness between. In the ice-fields, it chirruped warmly of sunshine; in the desert heat, it let drip notes of icy cool. Both landscapes understood, and showed they did by beginning to moderate. A rain fell on the ice-land, which should have been snow before it left the clouds; dry thunder crossed the aridity of the hilltop. More and more often the bird flew one way and the other, bringing cool to the unbearable heat, warmth to the intolerable cold. It stood on the surface of the frozen lake then flew to the summit of the dusty hill. In its tiny feet, the desert felt traces of ice-moisture, and the lake sensed the grit of a few sand-particles. Soon, the landscapes showed that they, too, were capable of movement. The hilltop stood taller, newly resistant to wind-erosion. The flat surface of the lake began to bow, to bend upwards. Something was there: a force beneath the pale surface.

The first crack of the ice was almost as violent a split as that of the entire planet. If any lovers had been slogging through the snow, pack-wearing, husky-following, they would have thought it a new apoca-lypse. A thunder-like rumble followed swiftly on from the lightning-like crash. Perhaps this half-planet was no longer a stable entity; perhaps gravity would have something to say about an implosive future. But within a few instants it became clear that the tumultuous noise had issued from the frozen lake rather than the wider landscape. The previously flat-as-flat surface, eased by the breaking, continued to swell upwards.

After the crack, the season had begun instantly to change from frigid winter to tremulous spring. The alteration was both sudden and gradual; sudden had been the bang of the new mood; gradual, the appearance of the specific details of it. A knowledge, however, from the first moment was in the air – a knowledge amounting to prophecy: *Again there would be colour! Once more, there would be life!*

Time, now, was very hard to gauge, but the growth was very gradual; a matter of months rather than hours and days, five perhaps or six. And during this period, the half-planet performed the emergence into spring. Droplets began to form, bejewelling the teensy tips of the icicles – then these began to drip – at first occasionally, then intermittently and finally incessantly. It was the drum-roll of thaw. Water ran over ice and helped persuade it to become water again, join in the downwards flow. The rime parted to allow the sun to witness this – and the bird chirruped of faraway warmth that knew of cold and was willing it to end. The monotone of the white landscape was prinked and rent with dots of green. Boulders reappeared, downhill from their old positions; tufts bravely stuck themselves through to re-begin the glorious task of photosynthesis. Almost before it seemed possible, the snow was all run-off and the landscape far and wide was a shaggy, flattened, brownish-green of previously oppressed but now liberated grasses. With a few more visits of the heat-singing bird, these began to regenerate. Brighter patches appeared, joined, overtook, completed their domination. And then buds with fistlike heads, like a crowd in silent revolution, stuck up a finger's-width above the grass. Thousand upon thousand, and all across the landscape, to the very water's edge, as never naturally before. Because of this, and because of their sheeny green, the buds appeared as an unprecedented amazement. After the not *blankness* but difference-of-detail of the ice and snow, they were a fresh kind of visual propulsion – something forgotten, so not truly new, and yet thrusting with the promise of truly renewed life. It was, to begin with, as if nothing had ever lived this vividly before – too glorious a spectacle to be merely Spring; it was resurrection from death, as if there had been a true chance of eternal non-existence.

The arrival of a different generation was unmistakable, even though there was no-one around but the bird to witness it – the bird which was now definitely a nightingale, and no longer the mania of the dawn chorus or the schizo-chaos of lark-becoming-blackbird-becoming-sparrow-becoming-lark, as before.

Each stem carried the head of an eye for the sun, and the lake-sun looked down – it came in close, and saw the blooming, and understood what it meant, and was desolated and proud and terrified. The lake-moon came, too – she was watery, through the clouds; a sliver, not an orb. Her close presence was an attempt to draw the waters of the lake out – to make them follow in total obedience. But if the gravity of the sun could not work upon the swelling lake, the relative unmassiveness of the moon was always going to fail.

Eventually, having survived some minor buffets of wind and blows of hail, the flowers stood ready to open. They were an army now, and although the opalescent tint of their sepals gave some hint as to their proper future hue, a secrecy of sorts was still possible. Millions of them were raised by stalks in the air, like heads, like fists, and then once more the nightingale sang – and, as if in response, the millions opened themselves, like faces, like hands – and what they brought to the world was a spreading gift of blue. The sky looked down upon a reflection of itself, and saw it not in the domelike waters of the lake but all across the landscape. It was an incredibly gentle blue, the colour that sorrow would be, if sorrow were a colour. Flowers ran from the lakeside to the far plains, right up to the very edge of the world where, if their petals fell, which they would, they would fall away for ever into emptiness.

The landscape was now a sublime combination of the tiny (the flowers themselves) and the grand (their colour) – the grand being composed of countless of the tiny, unevenly spread; the tiny, by similarity, partook every little one of the magnitude of the grand. There were grey-green gaps visible between the petals, but it seemed as if everything were now absolute blue or at least tinged to near-perfect blueness by reflected light. All, that is, except the surface of the lake, which – now a tall dome still continuing to bow outwards – kept a core of mysterious crimson. Movement, too, could be seen inside the crimson, had there been any to witness it.

The flowers had their strange season; it lasted longer than blooms normally do, but it came in the end to an end. The blue paled and yellowed and shrivelled, but the grass beneath the flowers had, by this time, renewed – and the loss of petals was the gain of stems. Green-bright was this new version of the world. All the landscape seemed to centre around the hill-like dome of the lake. The moon came and saw the movement beneath the surface – huge movement – and went away terrified. The sun no longer visited. The nightingale – the definite nightingale – sang of deserts turning green and fruitful.

And then the earth of the western half of the planet began to shudder. There was thunder without lightning and a juddering of rocks from sheer air-noise. All along the middle of the lake, from one side to the other, a jagged fissure appeared in what had seemed to be water. Side-cracks branched off from this central one, forming what would have looked from above like two giant sets of teeth. Tremors traversed the surface of the earth, all the way from its true equator to the edge of its cruel bisection. Shockwaves were felt as far away from the Lake District as the single pole. The very sky seemed troubled; more lowering than thunderstormy – *thunderstorm* was inadequate for this; it was maelstrom, it was apocalypse; implosion fighting explosion. The first gush from within was a spurt of icy water, near-frozen, then another, then one more. Wider and wider the crack-gap-crack gaped, and then a wide curve appeared beneath the skidding ice. It was blue and already obviously imperfect, or at least unusual. A huge force from within the lake-planet was pushing it from behind. Was this a volcanic moment? The sun and moon were in the sky, but far away, the moon partly eclipsing the sun. The landscape around gave a huge heave; the edges of the lake, the very shores, began to be ripped asunder – what was emerging seemed almost to be larger than what it was emerging from.

All the planet began to shudder. Rumblings and

boomings came from over the horizon, where, it was clear, the effects and anguish of all this were rightly being felt. There was no birdsong, however; the nightingale, to the western planet's disappointment, was not present; perhaps it was flying over the eastern hemisphere, silently, or sitting somewhere alone, playing with its hands.

The water-turned-ice was now swept entirely from the lake, and the dome of its surface had been replaced by the circumference of a new, odd planet.

For a moment it seemed as if the landscape would entirely shatter and be destroyed under this intolerable stress. Winds came and went, changing every second – reversing direction, towards the lake and away; towards, away. The light went blood-red. If pain, this was unbearable; if tension, intolerable; if creation, miraculous. For the lakesides gave, the landscape split, the ice broke, and up from the half-world, out of the maimed earth, swooned a new planet, small but with a gravity all its own.

This new planet was unpeeled into the world. It suffered a different gravity; not the lake-planet's – and so was able to move away from the lake-bed without difficulty and without choice. For just a few instants, the very bed of the lake was open to the air – visible to the moon in the sky, who had her memories also, and to the sun, who had instead his terrors. The lake bottom was not empty, but crawling with writhing-flopping-dying things that were not fish – suffocating in the air. Their skins were mottled and knobbly. But almost immediately, these horrors were covered over by the influx of water.

The sun shone brightly upon the new planet, with a dark light that had never before been seen – a crimson that was extremely harsh. By contrast, the moon went as pale as she had ever been: she appeared as if seen through watery clouds; as if light were weeping off her edges, as mist or steam. Then, all of a sudden, she waned to a sliver and fell like a petal might be expected to fall, downwards but also sideways – revolving not out of the turbulence of the air but out of a desire to be seen to swoon.

The new planet gave a few shallow breaths followed by a loud, high, ragged cry, its equator opening as a mouth and the mouth being the gummy wailing wet mouth of a little baby boy who, in being born, destroyed one universe and created another. Celeste, the mother-no-longer-a-planet, looks at her baby and sees that something is wrong with him, not very wrong, but wrong.

**II**

They are cutting the umbilical cord when the Captain enters the delivery suite, accompanied.

'The name,' he says. Then, before Celeste has a chance to open her mouth. 'You will have to choose a name.'

'I have,' she says. 'Orphan.'

The Captain stares at her, as if his stare alone will force her to speak another name. But when she keeps her silence, he says, 'You can't call it Orphan.'

'He's a boy, not an it,' says Celeste.

'He's a disgrace, and he will not be called Orphan. He has two parents.'

'Where is his father?'

The baby was waahing.

'His father could not be here – he could not be trusted to be here.'

'Because – what?' She implies the sexual act that the Captain does not mention.

The Captain stands to attention. He is more aware than usual of the eyes of the world.

'Do you intend self-harm?'

'I intend to call my son Orphan.'

'We will ask the child's father for a name.'

He steps across to where the baby boy is being weighed.

'Hmm,' he says, then leaves.

*

The Captain goes straight to Hydroponics, where he knows August will be. He asks the father for a name, then he pauses and says, 'Congratulations, I suppose.'

'When can I see him?' asks August. He is still transported by news of the safe birth but he is still furious at being denied the chance to even watch.

'Soon,' the Captain says. 'We just need a name.'

August says, 'What does Celeste want to call him?'

'But we want to know what *you* would like him called,' the Captain says.

'Call him whatever Celeste wants to call him. He's her son.'

'But he's *your* son, too.'

'She should name him. I wasn't even there. You wouldn't even let me be there.'

'Don't you have any ideas at all?'

'Celeste is the one,' he says.

In the end, they feel compelled to accept *Orphan* as his name – and Celeste's point is made permanent.

On hearing her choice, August cries.

'Yes,' he says. 'She always knows.'


Several hours later, Hubble – continuing in his role of go-between – is given permission to carry Orphan from Celeste's apartment to August's.

Until now, August has only been allowed to see Orphan via *it*, in a still image. Celeste's fingertips were visible, cradling the white blanket; the rest of her had been cropped out.

Passing the guard, Hubble enters, and hands the bundle over to August – who has been waiting by the door.

For the first time, the father looks down at his son.

Orphan's face is almost perfectly round; there is no chin to interrupt the smooth curve of its circumference. The two green eyes towards the middle of this circle bulge, but in a way that suggests constant keenness rather than any abnormality. His mouth, just below the eyes, is also circular, with a round pink tongue sticking out of it, wet and bubble-blowing. And, squeezed into the centre of this tight triangle of features is his nose; this is puggy.

'I know I'm meant to say he's the most beautiful thing I've ever seen,' says August, his eyes starry with tears. 'And, yes, that is what I want to say. He is. I'm not disappointed.'

'Why should you be?' asks Hubble.

'Because he's wrong, isn't he? Everyone's always going to think he shouldn't have been born.'

Hubble wants to say it is August who is wrong. However, news of Orphan's birth, and then of his naming, has not been well received by the crew. Many of them had argued for a termination as soon as the pregnancy was discovered. Australia had been one of the most passionate. 'He'll just be a drain on limited resources,' he had said, with all the confidence of sixteen healthy years. 'What will he ever do?'

'He will be loved,' Hubble had replied.

'By who? Who will love him?'

'I will,' said Hubble.

And despite being able to watch Orphan now, people's minds are not changed. Of course, no-one says that he should be killed. But when initial tests on his heart show some problems – holes, circular – a few think he might die naturally.

'It wouldn't be a bad thing,' says Australia. 'He wouldn't suffer much.'

The Chief Medical Officer, however, announces that the heart can be repaired, in a series of operations. Afterwards, when Orphan reaches maturity, it can be replaced when a donor organ becomes available.

As if to make up for the hate surrounding him, Celeste loves Orphan totally, from the very first moment. (And because August has been kept from her so completely, she has an extraordinary amount of love.) She finds everything Orphan does delightful. It isn't much. He sleeps, he wakes; he looks, he shudders; he cries for a short while, he feeds, he burps, he smiles, he sleeps. After a few weeks, he begins to smile whenever he isn't sleeping or feeding. And then, aged seven months, he starts to make wordlike sounds – *a-woo, a-goo*.

For most of this time, Celeste keeps Orphan alone with her in the apartment. She takes him out for walks – a buggy has been loaned to her – but avoids other people as much as she can; and they in return, as she senses, avoid her and her child.

As she walks, she reconsiders what they have done, together, August and her. She knows for certain that it was something wrong, but she also knows it was something for which they should not bear sole responsibility. Celeste now sees them as symptoms; it didn't matter that she was her and he was him, what mattered was the structure within which the whole crew was expected to exist. August and her had been forced into doing what they did by the intolerable sexual conditions of life on board. Incest was inevitable, sooner or later, given the privations of a hundred-person crew. Onboard resources were sufficient only for a crew of exactly that size. Whenever an older person died, a vacancy was created and – after much lobbying and resentment – was filled. As a system, it was very badly thought out. But applications to Mission for it to be relaxed were always rejected. The rules were fixed. Only the first two generations had been allowed to sexually reproduce amongst themselves. After this, everyone was meant to choose some smiling on-screen donor. If circumstances had been different, she and August would never have come together in the way they had. They had not felt star-crossed; star-thwarted, rather. Celeste could easily imagine loving other men, if only there had been other men to love, other men worth loving.

The paradox was, if she could have had her way, then none of them would be alive; Mission would never have been launched. It was all too early: the governments should have waited until cryonics technologies had advanced – until the crew could be unconscious throughout the whole journey. But what of the psychological consequences of this? Imagine arriving at the new home planet, sending off a message of triumph, only to discover, ten years later, that there was no-one left alive on Earth to receive it.

It is only when Orphan reaches a year, and has progressed from crawling to walking, that Hubble suggests he might like the company of other children.

Orphan's quiet little first-birthday party, with only himself and Celeste attending, had prompted Hubble to speak out.

There are three toddlers around Orphan's age, and they meet each morning in the playroom appropriate for them. Mission had incorporated five such playrooms into the design of Vessel – widely separated, so the older children couldn't bully the younger, and the younger couldn't pester the older. Celeste agrees to take Orphan along, if Hubble will prepare the way. She knows that, sooner or later, her son will have to begin mixing with others; this introduction might be the least painful. Apart from her, the only people he has played with are Hubble and August. Even her mother has not come near.

The following morning, Hubble approaches the three mothers: Irene, the Captain's daughter-in-law, Kaysha, the Communications Officer's Wife, and Atima, wife of Vladimir the Chemist. As they listen, they make slightly disgusted faces.

'But we don't know what he's like,' Irene says. 'He might be rough.'

'And it might upset the other babies,' says Kaysha. 'They're so used to one another now.'

'It would be good if you could make them welcome,' says Hubble. 'They are coming tomorrow.'

'Couldn't it be next week?' asks Atima. 'I mean, then we could be properly ready.'

Hubble doesn't ask what preparations they might need to make.

'At the start of next week, then,' he says, and goes to tell Celeste, who has been watching.

'They don't want him,' she says, holding Orphan on her knee although he is bucking to escape.

'Try it,' says Hubble. And when the day arrives, he comes along to make sure that she does.

The moment is far more difficult for the mother than for the son. He just gives a squeal of unaffected delight and starts stroking the feet of the nearest child, Vladimir and Atima's daughter, Minnow. Celeste, however, is reluctant to engage.

'How are you?' she is asked.

'We're both very good,' she replies. 'Thank you.'

The four women look at their children; Hubble stands by the gated door. Orphan has begun to giggle at the wriggling toes – they are so small; he has only ever seen his mother's toes.

'Orphan's a big boy, isn't he?' Kaysha says. 'Big for his height, I mean.'

In truth, Orphan is small and fat – mainly due to enforced inactivity.

'I don't know,' says Celeste. 'Is he?'

Minnow starts to giggle, so Orphan strokes her feet harder. He has just invented tickling.

This draws the attention of Irene's daughter, Penelope, and Boo, daughter of Kaysha. They laugh together for a while. Then a small hand grabs Orphan by his black hair and one of the girls tries to drag him across the floor.

'Penelope!' shouts her mother, then hurries over to intervene. Once she has her daughter up in her arms, Irene turns to Celeste and says, 'I'm so sorry. She doesn't know what she's doing.'

Orphan, who has hardly noticed, is already up on

his feet and running towards Penelope. He wants her to rejoin the play.

Hubble decides that he can now safely leave.


Although Orphan's three playmates accept him immediately, it takes their mothers a little longer. But once they have a chance to see how instinctively gentle and unfailingly happy the little boy is, and how much he likes their daughters, they are soon on his side – defending him against those who, aware of goings-on in the first playroom, argue that Orphan should be kept separate.

'For how long? If he doesn't join in, he'll never learn anything.'

'He's not to blame for how he is. Why should he be punished?'

'The girls would miss him terribly if he suddenly disappeared.'

The grandmothers and grandfathers – including the Captain – pay especially close attention to Orphan's behaviour around their dear ones, and are also won over by his round little beamishness.

Gradually, the overall attitude of the crew begins to change. Orphan, aged two, is amusing, clownish. He can certainly be tolerated – outside the playroom as well as in. Even when he causes it, he means no harm.

August and Celeste, however, are still ostracized.

Almost as soon as August is permitted to leave his apartment, he makes his way down to Hydroponics, where food for everyone – vegetables and fruit – is grown. To begin with, he just spends time wandering up and down the bays. But it isn't long before he asks whether he can help out with cultivation. The question is referred to the Captain, who replies positively. After this, August is only rarely seen on the upper decks – walking to and from his living quarters. He eats straight from the plant, so avoids the mess hall. When it is seen that he is making himself useful, people grunt and say that it is just as well, given the trouble he's caused.

What August doesn't want is decisions; it pleases him obediently to carry out any request made by the Head Gardener, Yarrow, seven years his junior. There is no weeding – there are no weeds; also, there are no pests. At launch, the vessel had been a hermetically sealed environment. And, anyway, the strains it carries are the most advanced ever developed. Even so, with inherited caution, the crop varieties are rotated every three years. The growth of each plant is predictable but always surprising: August watches them closely, knowing this shoot as it becomes this bud and this leaf – and, sometimes, this salad.

Early on, August likes to think that although people might not open their mouths to speak to him, they will still do so to eat the food he has grown. He wants to be as generous as he can. It does not occur to him that he might be turning fatherly towards the crew: wishing to provide for their most basic needs.

Attitudes to Celeste, who is far more despised, hardly change at all. The mothers in the playroom, now Playroom-2, talk to her, but only about Orphan. He is leader of the little gang. He has the most energy and he plays with the greatest passion. If he gets upset and difficult, it is almost always when the game has to end – either because the girls are bored or because they have to leave.

As Orphan's third birthday comes around, August makes a surprise request – he wants to be permitted to attend the party. He makes his approach, in person, direct to the Captain, who says he will think the matter over.

'I have been no trouble,' says August, 'generally.'

'I realize that,' the Captain replies. 'I will take that into consideration.'

'Thank you, sir,' says August, and retreats. He looks unnervingly thin.

It is now almost thirty years since the Captain, Abd al-Salaam, took command of Vessel. He is a vigorous, bald and shiny-headed man. His armpits smell of salt, and he spends much of his free time exercising in the gym, or repairing the gym equipment he has broken. Recently, he has begun to think of stepping aside. The routines of command have become monotonous: the daily reports to Control, Control's constant outdated feedback. He hopes that his son, Aladdin, will be mature enough to take over. And it is with this in mind that he consults him on the issue of Orphan's birthday party.

'No,' says Aladdin. 'He must be refused.'

'Why do you think that?' the Captain asks.

'People wouldn't like it. They don't want to see them together again. It reminds them.'

'Of what? Of my great mistake?'

They are in Aladdin's apartment, where the walls are set to crimson and gold. Abd al-Salaam has come on the pretext of visiting Penelope, his grand-daughter. But she is at this moment being put to bed, and the men are alone.

'It wasn't a mistake,' says Aladdin. 'If it was any-thing, it was a collective negligence.' The phrase comes easily. He has often, in his head, argued against his father's critics. Aladdin knows there will have been many of them, on Earth.

'In fifteen months, we'll hear the reaction from Control. They won't be happy.'

'Someone should have reported what was going on to you – or their parents.'

The Captain takes a sip of water, swallows it.

'The question still remains. Is there any reason to keep August from celebrating his son's birthday?'

'He can celebrate it,' says Aladdin. 'He can celebrate it on his own. With his plants.'

August is already something of a joke: the beard, the eyes.

'No,' says the Captain. 'He can be trusted, I think, to behave himself. He's a changed man. He's a man. Everyone will be watching him.'

'But won't it appear as if we're forgiving him?'

'A longer-term solution also needs to be worked out. What do you suggest?'

'I suggest no change from the present arrangement.'

Abd al-Salaam looks at his son, fully assessing him.

'There is no such thing as no change. August and Celeste will be allowed to be together –'

Aladdin begins to interrupt.

'Not as lovers, of course. But . . .' says the Captain.

'But they will have to agree to certain conditions.'

'What conditions?'

The Captain goes towards the door. 'We will consult with the crew. Let them decide.'

'What if the crew don't want them together at all? What if they forbid it?'

'That decision has already been made. Kiss Penelope good night for me.'

The Captain leaves.

At the next briefing, the conditions are debated and decided. They turn out to be extremely harsh – an expression of the crew's continuing animus towards the cousins (who are, as usual, not present). Australia it is who makes the first suggestion of a medical solution.

If August will submit to a vasectomy and Celeste to a hysterectomy, then they will be allowed once again to be alone in one another's company – but never in the tennis courts or the showers.

On hearing this, August says he has no objections but that he thinks Celeste will. He is understating, as he always does. Celeste is inconsolable – and tells Hubble, who has hurried straight from the meeting, to go away.

'What, Mummy?' asks Orphan.

She has to lock herself in the bedroom, so that he only hears her crying through the door.

'Silly Mummy,' Orphan says.

For five minutes, Celeste weeps.

'I refuse,' she says, when she can speak. 'I utterly refuse.' She knows that her words will be heard.

After this, August makes no attempt to persuade or contact her. Celeste will never accept such terms.

On the day before the birthday party, the Captain intervenes. August will be granted special dispensation for a single visit of no longer than three hours.

'Hello,' says August.

'Hello,' says Celeste. 'Come in.'

'Thank you,' says August.

'Hello,' says Hubble.

Hubble has long brown curly hair and a nose that looks twice as wide as it should be. August has seen him via *it*, but in person he is still shockingly, shamblingly adolescent.

August enters Celeste's strange apartment, and is surprised to find it so quiet. He has been expecting a party, something much louder than Hydroponics. Penelope, Minnow and Boo are absent; they, and their parents, were invited, but the adults still did not feel able to attend. To do so would be to celebrate Orphan's birth, and no-one apart from his parents and Hubble is yet prepared to be seen doing that.

'Please sit down,' says Celeste.

'Thank you,' says August.

For the next two hours, they do not address one another directly again – everything goes through Orphan, who is almost hallucinating with excitement. They know this scene is being watched, or will be watched, by everyone on board – and afterwards by billions back on Earth. It makes them more than self-conscious.

August wishes he could be silent and invisible, yet still present, still able to play I'm-going-to-drop-you with his son.

Celeste tries not to wish for anything; she thinks that, if she appears to have desires, they will be thwarted. Being in the same room as August, after the intensity they had reached before, is a worse punishment than separation. Celeste tries to glance at him, the co-creator of the world, the father of her child, without actually looking – almost fulfilling his wish not to be seen. It is terrible: he is so ordinary, without aura. Of all things, she hadn't expected that.

Still, she needs to speak, and eventually she does. Orphan is playing with his new toy, a hand-me-down race-car already battered by several previous generations of children. Hubble is supplying noises of acceleration and skidding.

'I would like to go for a walk,' says Celeste.

August gets up off the floor, where he has been helping Orphan drive. He thinks Celeste means immediately – a walk immediately. But their agreement with the Captain doesn't allow them out of her quarters.

'Sit down,' she says.

He finds a chair.

'I mean a long walk,' says Celeste. 'On my own. I feel so ...'

Then August knows she means suicide – the part-fulfilling of the prophecy of Orphan's name. With *it* listening to their every word, analysing, reporting, Celeste has had to invent a euphemism. If she had explicitly spoken of suicide aloud, their meeting would have been broken up within seconds. As things stood, there was always the chance that those others watching would understand, and report them. August listens for the approach of guards.

'That would be nice,' he says. 'A walk. But where is there to go?'

'I may try to explore.'

Celeste is pleased, even in the midst of her despair: she had known she could trust August, still – of all the men aboard, he is by far the most emotionally intelligent. Orphan picks up faster on her moods, but is merely annoyed by them: her mood must be *his* mood. Tears make him laugh. August, though, has always known when to approach her and when to absent himself.

'Are you certain you want to go on your own?'

'Yes,' she says. 'I think so.'

They do not hate one another – what they feel, he assumes (and she, secretly, too) is still more akin to passionate love. The truth is that Celeste finds it unbearable to be in the same space as August; all his futile tenderness, leaning forwards, is a suffocation. He, for his part, wants more than anything to sit talking with her – for years, for the remainder of his life. August feels anguished at the idea of her death. But he also wants her to have what she wants, whatever it is.

Of course, even though *it* has been eluded, many of the other watchers understand exactly what Celeste is saying. They know she will have anticipated this, too. And so her melancholy words are taken as an explicit threat, rather than an expression of weariness and lack of hope.

'Goodbye,' says Celeste.

'Goodbye,' says August.

Afterwards, to cover herself, Celeste leaves Orphan with Hubble and goes for a short walk.

Following the party, August expects for weeks to hear that Celeste is no more. But the news doesn't come. She keeps alive, and he has no idea why.

In truth, Celeste is too fascinated by her son to leave him.

Four and a quarter years after Orphan's birth, the Captain receives the expected message. He is, with immediate effect, suspended from his post. The Vice-Captain, who has received notification two hours earlier, takes command of Vessel. Abd al-Salaam is escorted to his quarters.

After it had become known on Earth what had transpired between August and Celeste, a military tribunal was set up. Even though its decision is now a couple of years in the past, and they are millions of kilometres away, Abd al-Salaam will have to wait out their judgement as if in real time.

Aladdin is allowed to visit his father.

'They can't do anything, if we decide to ignore them.'

'Mission appointed me. If they no longer want me to be Captain, then I have no other authority.'

'You have our authority – the authority of the crew. They want you to continue. I'm sure they do.'

And, even in the short while since Abd al-Salaam's deposition, a general rallying round has taken place.

The argument goes like this: The Captain had done nothing wrong – nothing that any of them wouldn't have done, under the same circumstances. Who among them could have known what was taking place between August and Celeste? Ever since their day-apart births, everybody had expected them to be the closest of friends. This was what their mothers, Stella and Astra, had hoped for. And because of the unusually intimate blood-relations between their parents, the crew had – without realizing it – gone beyond friendship, even coming to regard August and Celeste as brother and sister. And siblings knew that there were limits to the intimacy they were allowed. August and Celeste had known.

But should they have been spied upon every minute of the waking day? Should they have been forcibly separated, as they were after the discovery?

The crew now feel themselves to be people of a different order to those on Earth. Perhaps they have been ever since the long-gone day of the launch.

In setting out for Planet Aurora, they were truly attempting to create a new society – one more generous and harmonious than the old.

A meeting is called, in the Great Hall, and Aladdin speaks out on his absent father's behalf. It is expected that he will find no opposition, but Australia steps forward. His eyes are large.

'If we proceed in this manner, Mission will find ways of punishing us.'

'How could they do that?' Aladdin asks.

'They could deny us basic information. They could deny us any information at all.'

'And put the mission in jeopardy? I don't think so.'

'Your father himself argued that he should not challenge the will of Mission.'

'I know that he will return as Captain, if the crew wants him to return. Do you want my father to be Captain?'

*it* performs an instantaneous sound and vision analysis. The result is displayed: 98 per cent of those present have said *Yes*.

Abd al-Salaam is released from his captivity and, with great delight, escorted back to the command deck. He tries to resist, but popular opinion will not let him. The Vice-Captain gladly steps aside, saying, 'You are our Captain. You will remain as our Captain.'

*Thank you, my friends* is all he says.

It is received as a great speech, worthy of ovation.

A few days later, the tribunal's message arrives. On consideration, it says, the Captain will not be court-martialled, nor will he be replaced. He can remain in post, though with a severe black mark on his record.

The crew laugh as they watch the serious old men in their colourful uniforms. They are so far away. They are so wrong.

It might be thought that, given these events, there would be some relaxation in the attitude of condemnation towards August and Celeste, but the crew is just as capable of hypocrisy as any other human society.

If anything, as affection for Orphan increases, until it becomes almost the defining characteristic of the vessel, so does the scapegoating of his parents. They receive no love-dividend; Orphan takes it all – perhaps because he is about the only outlet for charity on board, especially now that the last of the first generation has died. (Mrs Woods' unit is cleared out. Those moving in report that the almond smell still, mysteriously, remains strong – and, in fact, it will do so until the ship comes to its end.)

'Boo,' says Orphan, and everyone laughs and acts surprised, as if they hadn't heard him thumping up behind them, hadn't heard afar off his snorty, over-excited breathing.

In games with Penelope, Minnow and Boo, Orphan doesn't mind being the scary space monster – he *wants* to be the scary space monster: roaring, charging, tickling, mating. He would willingly spend his whole life this way – and perhaps, in a sense, that is what he is finally allowed to do.


Hate-mails for Celeste start arriving shortly after the Captain is reappointed.

Reports of her and August's incest had been kept out of the media until the tribunal came to a decision. After that, everyone on Earth learnt of it.

They were the most intense news story for a whole week, something quite unprecedented. Celeste's address – along with August's – was read out in churches, temples, mosques. Religions she has never heard of execrated and excommunicated the two of them; and all their hundreds of thousands of followers condemned her *specifically*: the woman was always more to blame. It was for her to say *no*.

With horror, Celeste reads maybe a hundred of the initial wave, and knows from them what the others will say. Whore. Unnatural. Bitch. Hell. The death threats almost make her laugh, so ridiculous are they; as if the senders might somehow be able to get close enough to harm her. But there is, Celeste realizes, always the possibility that someone on board might be tempted to become a hero, albeit a murderous one.

'We are civilized,' says the newly reinstated Captain, in an attempt to forestall this. 'We must not allow a barbarous act to tempt us into barbarism.'

Celeste's supporters on Earth terrify her almost as much as those who simply feel disgust. The positive messages she receives are most of them pornographic in content.

Celeste breaks down. She orders *it* to stop notifying her of mail, which has become a constant wail of beeps; she does not even want a total-count, which is well over ten million by the third day.

At a stroke, she and August had become among the most infamous human beings ever born. Their behaviour had given the divided peoples of a fractious planet at least one thing to agree upon, or so it seemed. They would always be thought of together: Adam and Eve, Paolo and Francesca, Bonnie and Clyde: sinner couples.

The feeling of all this hate directed towards her slowly begins to corrode Celeste. And this at a moment when, on board, some of the younger comrades are secretly becoming fascinated with her. How could they not? She is such a forbidden subject, and so few subjects are obviously forbidden.

Celeste's bitterness, as it appears to her new admirers, is a bizarrely, paradoxically beautiful thing – bitterness should never be beautiful, but Celeste somehow manages to make hers that, or, at least, through her charisma and demeanour, to make it *appear* that. Bitterness seems to chill the air around her. Aboard, the healthy psychologies are all so similar that even her glacial desolation is some relief. For those who have never seen snow or experienced sub-zero temperatures, a conversation with Celeste, even a word, is the closest thing.

It does not take long before she has become a firm cult among the adolescents.

They observe her, both in person and through *it*. Although this agonizes her, and increases her bitterness, the Captain refuses to block them. She *should* be surveyable; her negative example is there to be learnt from. When she'd done what she'd done (he avoids the word *incest*), she had forfeited her right to privacy. Her temperature decreases yet further.

August, by contrast, becomes saturnine; he is the dog days falling anywhere, not a specific or consciously mimicked place on Earth – and not exactly despairing, but with an inescapable lassitude. He wants to give up. He wants especially to give up trying to give up. Every year, without fail, he attends Orphan's birthday party. For the rest of the time, however, he isn't much seen.

Celeste tries to stop herself telling Orphan she loves him – at least, in other people's hearing. They resent, she knows, her being so intimate with him. It is absurd, but they would like to give him another mother; and, in as much as they can, they do: they *all* adopt him, overwhelming him with a hundred parents.

It is hard to know when Orphan first begins to sense he is something out of the ordinary, something quite especially special.

The main sign of this is that people like him more than they like other people, and because liking is the element in which he has always consciously moved, he doesn't sense it as anything other than natural.

Slowly, Orphan becomes aware that there are rules he is allowed to break which Penelope, Minnow and Boo are not – the unheralded visits to the bridge, for example.

The girls do not resent Orphan for this; their anger is directed at the grown-ups who, by letting him do as he does, give glimpses of a better state of affairs. Orphan is a pioneer, without intending or even suspecting it, a moral pioneer. In this, he is supported by his generation: they know that, gaily as he goes, leaving behind him on the floor shiny blips of drool, Orphan is forcing changes – creating new freedoms which, one day, will be theirs; they will *make* them theirs.

As everyone has for a while been expecting, the Captain does step aside. He wishes to allow his son, Aladdin, now aged forty, to take command. Aladdin, he believes, has reached maturity.

Due procedure is followed; the meeting is quorate; no nepotism is involved as none is necessary: the

Captain's son is simply the most Captainlike man aboard – and, in this, being the son of the Captain gives him all the advantage he needs: he looks just like a Captain should; he looks just like his father looked when *he* became Captain.

The only person seriously to resent this transition is Australia, who, aged twenty-five, is far too young – except in his own head – to become Captain.

Australia will be next; that is the general belief. Penelope, the Captain's grand-daughter, will not be old enough to take over for several decades. Australia will mark time.

This untroubled succession gives Vessel a feeling of stability and also potentiality. The Captain's son becomes the new Captain; the Captain becomes the ex-Captain. This is as it should be.

But, shortly afterwards, something else happens. Orphan is paying one of his sudden visits to the bridge. It amuses him to pretend he is steering the ship, although it has no manual controls, as such. He drives it like his race-car, which he still often plays with. The Astrogation Officer lets Orphan think he is directing Vessel, until he loses interest and goes away again.

Although he has been told repeatedly that Aladdin is the Captain, Orphan doesn't seem to believe it; and when someone addresses Aladdin this way, Orphan shouts out: 'No! No!' It looks for a moment as if he is about to have one of his fits. They are just thinking about having the boy carried to Celeste when he starts giggling.

'I the Captain,' he says. 'Not he. I the Captain. Say me Captain! Say me the Captain, now!'

Everyone on the bridge immediately and smilingly obeys his order.

'Yes, Captain,' they say. 'Certainly, Captain.'

And so naturally does this happen that no-one present, and there are quite a few officers and others, thinks this is really the first time.

Orphan – in his own mind – has always been Captain, from the moment he realized such a position existed. Orders are his favourite way of speaking: *Stop!* And *Give it!* And *Dark away!* And *Shut up! Shut up!*

Even Aladdin feels no true disquiet at this funny moment. Orphan is never going to challenge him. Why not let him enjoy his illusion? But a major shift of power has, just then, irrevocably, taken place.

Some of the officers start to call Orphan *Captain* off the bridge as well as on – and, because it delights him so much, the habit spreads until it is general.

Within a week, the UNSS *Armenia* has two people who are addressed as *Captain* – and who is to say which of them receives that homage with the greater sense of entitlement and security?

Years pass, and Orphan – now thirteen – becomes aware of conversations going on a short distance above his head. (He has stopped growing, and will never become tall enough for them to be at his level.)

After the time of the word *Jerusalem*, which he pronounces *Jew-Slam*, there comes the time of the words which rhyme, *Negotiation, Reconciliation, Legislation* and *Celebration* (said by Orphan as *No-Shay-Shay, Wrestle Vacation, Less Less Asian* and *Zeb-Rayshun*). The Captain holds a party, and *that* – Orphan learns – is a Zeb-

Rayshun. The meanings of the other words continue to perplex and elude him.

When the Captain makes a speech, his toast is 'To Humanity'. Orphan knows this is a name – Jew-Slam No-Shay-Shay had been done in the name of Humanity (*Manatee*.)

Orphan never spots Manatee at the party, but he suspects it might be some food or a kind of light – something very nice for grown-ups.

When he asks his mother what Manatee is, she takes a while to understand but then laughs in a way that is more like coughing before being sick. 'Good question,' she says.

Orphan goes to the bridge and shouts-happy, calling for Manatee to come, so he can eat it or see it.

The Astrogation Officer brings up an image of a manatee, but Orphan is not satisfied.

After the Zeb-Rayshun, everything seems better – which makes Orphan wonder why they don't have parties all the time, to make everything keep on getting better.

He tells his mother, the next day, 'More Zeb-Rayshun, more Zeb-Rayshun.' And for several weeks afterwards will ask, 'Now Zeb-Rayshun?' She has to disappoint him.

But still he presses her, until she comes to believe he is becoming haunted by the idea of Jerusalem – this non-existent place that is so important to everyone around him. Celeste tries repeatedly to explain the history of the conflict and the importance of the recent peace. She shows Orphan maps and footage. He claps at the explosions. He giggles. He runs away. He seems incapable of focusing; to him, none of it is any more or less real than his favourite cartoons.

Frustrated, Celeste yearns to know how Earth exists for Orphan, in his solid head. Simplified, or so she thinks, and it would have to be as a very big version of the vessel – obviously; but she suspects he understands it better in terms of colour and texture than of shape and scale.

The idea that you might be in a place and not know everyone there, or have everyone there know you, is one he seems incapable of developing – and why force it upon him? For it remains true that, even if he were able instantly to visit Earth, every single person he met *would* know just who he was; would not, however, be his friend – might, in fact, attempt to harm him.

Even though they were impossibly far away, Celeste still feels, on Orphan's behalf, scared of these people – and furious towards them. To them, he was an abstraction, an abomination, to be condemned according to easy, inherited laws. To her, he is warmth and softness and the goodness innate in warmth and softness; he is humour when all else is devastation; he is her externalized and vulnerable heart, and anything that happens to him happens to her.

*We shouldn't be here* – that is the realization she fears Orphan will arrive at, one day. Never once has she mentioned the Lakes to him, for fear that he might conceive a desire to go there. If so, she would have to pretend it was the nickname of part of the ship – the water tanks. Her body feels different when she thinks of that time, the time with August – not more youthful but more aware of the feelings of youth which it no longer feels; in an anti-glow, she glows.

But Orphan never comes close to the thought *We shouldn't be here.* In this, Celeste has misunderstood his very essence: he is the first crew-member, and more grandiosely the first *human*, truly to exist without nostalgia for origins. He is *homo galacticus*; no longer chthonic, at heart.

The truth of him is, he makes *no* effort to understand their former homeworld, because it does not interest him. Nothing it could offer has any real appeal – not beaches or amusement parks, not confectionery or others like himself. Even animals are too abstract. All he cares about, and all he loves, is the vessel and, inside the vessel, the crew. The only experiences which mean anything to him are the ones he has already had, and these will always be available.

And then, utterly suddenly, there is no longer any homeworld to be understood or misunderstood. The question becomes irrelevant, or the most important question of all – for Earth, in their heads, becomes the only meaningful Earth left in existence. A sudden attack had been made, that much they can tell. There followed retaliation, retaliation to the retaliation, obliteration.

During the three days when this is becoming clear, Celeste stays in her room, not even stepping out into her apartment. She eats nothing, does not miss food, and is not sure if she will ever be bothered to eat anything again. Hubble brings her water, then goes to rejoin the wailing-terrified huddle in the mess hall. He feels the need for human embrace, and everyone is now constantly hugging everyone else: it becomes a mania, all that can be done or seems right to do.

Throughout this period of ultimate crisis, as the news arrives, worsens, and then stops arriving, the crew turn desperately to the Captain for leadership – and he speaks to them in the mess hall, saying all the appropriate things: *We do not yet know for absolute certain* and *Let us hope that there still* and *Let us join together in prayer*; then he breaks down. They are dealing, from now on, every moment, with the unthinkable – the unthinkable as a finished fact. Aladdin suffers a vastation; he becomes convinced that the vessel's hull has weakened, and that the airlessness outside is about to overtake them. At moments, he refuses to breathe, believing that the breach has already occurred, and that if he opens his mouth his insides will spill out. The crew observe their Captain, in his mania; his panic becomes theirs. The universe has suddenly expanded infinitely, and for all practical purposes, they are alone.

Abd al-Salaam goes to his son, speaks of the importance of self-control. Aladdin gathers himself again, publicly, aiming also to gather the crew, and says, or tries to say, how the importance of Mission is now even greater. 'For upon it depends the entire future of humanity.' The mess hall listens to him. But then, 'Manatee!' shouts Orphan, who is very happy that day. He loves the hugs; he loves being consoling. Although it has been repeatedly explained to him, he can't understand why the death of the Earth is such a tragedy.

After his speech, Aladdin collapses. He can do

nothing more than shiver and puke. His father, seeing no alternative, immediately takes over. Something practical needs to be done. And so he announces that in a few minutes' time he will be narrowcasting a message of solidarity to the Captains of the three other surviving ships – the UNSS *Afghanistan*, *Albania* and *Angola* – although everyone knows he and they will be dead by the time it is received and replied to.

The mess hall is awash with unprecedented emotion. It isn't exactly grief, because it is both too huge and too abstract for that, but it does resemble mourning, grief-stricken mourning, more closely than anything else. What they feel, all apart from Orphan, is a kind of supreme cosmic embarrassment: a foolish exposure in the presence of everything in existence, and everything that has ever existed, and everything that will ever exist; so much less, now.

Under such circumstances, to continue to think of oneself as human is a humiliation.

There has always been pride available, in the onwardness of their species-quest. Now, there is oblivion – deserved oblivion. The wall of total smash and end has been brought *that* much closer, and whatever the outcome is ultimately to be depends hugely upon them. 'We have to re-create,' says Abd al-Salaam, continuing his son's broken speech. 'We have the help of *it* – *it* updated until the very last moment of humanity's existence.'

'Manatee!' shouts Orphan, again. And this time Penelope, Minnow and Boo join in.

*We can no longer call it humanity.* That is August's

thought, although he doesn't voice it. *We have lost the right.*

'It is wrong to look for positives on the worst day of human history.' Abd al-Salaam speaks as if the destruction wasn't already over two years in the past – as if the hearing of the news were equivalent to the holocaust of the event. 'Much has been lost ...' Almost, he cannot continue. But if he collapses, as his son had, then the crew may utterly despair. Everything depends upon him.

He finds a way of going on. 'Much has been lost, much that is simply irreplaceable. And what we have lost, most of all, are the physical artefacts. But we still have the information. We may have lost the books, but we still have the words; we may have lost the paintings, but we still have the images; we may have lost the lives, but we still have the condensed meaning of those lives. We *embody* – that's what I'm trying to say. We embody.'

Ovation follows, dwindles.

A good speech, all agree, going from hug to hug; perhaps not a *great* speech, until time-passing makes it so: it has expressed accurately and beautifully what they are thinking. But it comes nowhere near to expressing what they are feeling – and, as a consequence, it fails completely to say what they want to hear said.

Then Orphan speaks, and everyone welcomes the likely irrelevance of it – or otherwise they think he might naively repeat Abd al-Salaam's words, showing that this is a total tragedy, universally understood.

'Let's have *Zeb-Rayshun*,' shouts Orphan. 'Party. Party fun now!'

And, as Aladdin drools on to his wife's collarbone, the suggestion is taken up, taken seriously. Just as at a funeral, and just as in the cliché, there is sadness for the life lost but also (and more so) celebration of the life lived. Orphan's logic, as August knew, is that the last party had made things better, and so this one will, too.

And, in a way, it does.

Alcohol rations are temporarily removed. It is important for a certain level of abandon to be achieved, and then for that abandon to be overtaken by oblivion. The crew go to their apartments, put on their best clothes, and return; many, without conference, bring back with them the most precious of their Earth-artefacts: a tortoiseshell tea-caddy with a soft silver crest for a lock, a Hannukah menorah with all nine of its candles lit, a ceramic cookie-jar in the shape of Homer Simpson, a diamond necklace (even this is votively carried, not worn). These are all placed in a circle around the edge of the Captain's table; instantly, a shrine is recognized. When people want to weep most deeply, here is where they bring themselves. Otherwise, they drink, hug, make toasts to the billions deceased, praise Orphan, drink more, fall into temporary silences.

Australia lies passed out under a common table – the death of the Earth has destroyed the existing grounds of his ambition; for who is there now to strut in front of and be praised by?

Aladdin seems almost to enjoy his temporary demotion to ordinary crew-member. He can rave as the mood takes him. Everyone knows that his father is once again in command; everyone also keeps the knowledge that the idea for the party had been neither Aladdin's nor Abd al-Salaam's but Orphan's: instinct, not authority, had brought them to the right place – and authority, on Earth, had been the cause of the end. In future, there might have to be changes, big changes. Yet, for the moment, all Orphan wants to do is dance – he loves dancing – and so *it*, encouraged by many, begins to broadcast Orphan's top fifty favourite songs.

For some reason, these happy ditties come out of every speaker in the ship. Celeste hears them in her room; immediately telling *it* to turn the volume down.

But the regular thumping is still out there in her kitchen and, beyond, all along the corridor.

Celeste guesses what it means; she has heard the tunes often enough before. Orphan's pleasures have always been obsessive and incessant – just as they will continue to be, right up until his death.

The leaves of the plants in Hydroponics vibrate slightly, as the bass frequencies pulse sideways through the air. August, however, isn't there but at the centre of whatever group is largest. For the first time since his disgrace, he is fully accepted.

Vladimir, down in the laboratories, has synthesized some more hexanal, some more grass; he inhales it until tears fall in lines beneath the hairs of his beard. Others, who have been fucking or standing at portholes staring off alone into space, hurry back to the mess hall and wholeheartedly join in. Vladimir, too, eventually returns. And when it becomes clear that *everyone* is there, dancing, everyone apart from Celeste, August is sent to fetch her.

No-one expects that she will come willingly. A group of male volunteers gather, intending to carry her roughly from her apartment if she won't walk. Already, they can feel the weight of her speculated body.

But then, holding hands with August, she appears in the doorway. Orphan sees them, gives a squeak of high joy and drags them off into the middle of the bounding mass.

The following day is bad; a new low. Hardly anyone has experienced a serious hangover before.

Vladimir, who over the past several years has synthesized pure alcohol for private use, goes around advising rest and rehydration. The ship's medical officers are occupied with those – mainly men – who believe they might be dying.

Even so, people feel better for the emotional release of the party. Though it had probably been meaningless, they had done *something* – they had found something to do; thanks, in main part, to Orphan, who is his usual perky self. The much-wine he had drunk does not seem to have affected him. In fact, he spends most of the day asking for more, and emptying down his thirteen-year-old throat any abandoned cups he happens to find.

Orphan is very disappointed, come evening, when no second party starts up. All his friends (of course, everyone is his friend) seem so sad; another party will make them happy again.

'No,' he is told. And then, 'Really, *no.*'

Orphan, as Captain, tries ordering them to have fun. But his authority has not yet reached the level of compulsion.

The mood is very different the following day, and the day after that. An existential crisis is forced upon even those who have, so far, shown few signs of a nuanced or turbulent interior life. Questions of metaphysics become overwhelming: *What do our lives mean without the planet of our origin? Should our morality alter, given that we are the only people alive to witness and judge our acts? Does the death of the Earth mean the death of the human? Are we, therefore, something other? And, if not, are we doomed to repeat the human fate, the human folly, and destroy ourselves?* The question which keeps returning, in one form or another, is this: *What is the meaning of something which is utterly gone?*

Those unused to philosophizing do so in a panicky rush, as if some breakthrough might be made in the next half-hour. Study groups are formed around particular epistemological, teleological and other questions: *So, what is the meaning of life, now? Do we know anything about anything any more? Are human beings innately evil? Does God exist – and, if so, does He hate us?*

Ecumenical gatherings, often consisting of the same fluttery souls, discuss whether the apocalypse of the Bible, Qu'ran, Torah, Vedas, etcetera, has, in fact, happened, and, if so, what the crew's theological position now might be.

This is not the end of the universe, rationalists meet to argue, but it is definitely the end of *a* universe – a universe to which they had, at the very least, been particularly attached.

Even practical questions become existential. Should everyone's rations be cut, in anticipation of scarcer times ahead? If rations aren't cut, does that make total extinction slightly more likely or completely inevitable? Does it matter to any of them that the human enterprise is perhaps drawing to a close? None now living would have survived to witness their arrival at the planet, and, even then, none of the generations who arrived would still have been alive to receive the message of congratulations from Mission Control.

Each of them – even before the catastrophe – had already come to some accommodation with the idea of personal extinction within the confines of the vessel. And now the definite possibility of species-death is superadded to that. How do the two things fit together? Do they make each individual life more important or less?

'There are only twice as many of us now, on board, as there were presidents of the United States of America. I am worth almost half a Commander-in-Chief.' So says Australia, who has quickly found reasons for recovery.

There is a great deal of both voluntary and involuntary medication; more sedatives than ever before are ordered to be synthesized. Vladimir works twenty-one-hour shifts.

One of the main difficulties the crew has to deal

with, existentially, is the notion that Earth had been dead for a full two and a half years before indications of this reached them. And so, clearly, it isn't the *fact* of its extinction but the *knowledge* of this fact that changes their universe.

Some comrades claim to have sensed something was wrong. They back-search their own dialogue and diaries, finding moments of unease, but no-one produces conclusive evidence of foresight, let alone prophecy. The truth is that, for most of them, the Jerusalem negotiations seemed to have achieved lasting peace – right up until a week before the end. Perhaps this makes the general breakdown even worse: there had been no preparation whatsoever.

In the first few days, everyone on board receives millions of messages; this, it seems, was how many on Earth had spent their final moments. They enclosed fragments-to-be-saved – novels they had begun, nature poems with missing middles, images still and moving of themselves as adults and as children, tax records with obscene spoken commentary. In panic and love, some had mailed off every single byte: entire lives were there, beamed into space, just in the hope someone on board would notice, spend a moment. It takes a while for the information to come through, there is so much: Abd al-Salaam and Aladdin are aware that, at the same time, *it* is receiving specially created UN files. Mission is now deeply altered, and background on civilization-building has been sent in more easily utilizable form.

The Upload, as it comes to be known, continues for

three days – mails arriving from those desperate that the trivia of their life, or its summary statement, not be lost.

Celeste is among those comrades interested, but her principle of search becomes to find only the smallest files. Often these contain a single image of the sender and a one-line message. A particularly memorable one is of an eighty-year-old Romanian woman: *Childless, happy now.*

Then there are others:

*'I dont kno if any one will ever read this but I am glad that I lived even tho that was only for such a short time (I was 18 this June 17th) and I wish I was more gennerous to my friends I love them but now it is almost over I just want someone to hold on to at the very end.'*

And:

*'I give my soul to Jesus, nobody else ever seemed to want the damn thing.'*

And:

*'The waste of it all just makes me want to weep – I am weeping.'*

The most common and clichéd line is *'Finally, really did it! You maniacs! You blew it up! Ah, damn you! God-damn you all to hell!'* – which was adapted from some film.

Celeste is moved and annoyed: people like this – good, anonymous people – they would never have brought the world to destruction, but someone had, and on their behalf.

*'Stop the madness!!!'*

*'I still hate that goddamn bitch.'*

*'We had a good innings.'*

'*I always knew this would happen I knew it I knew it.*'

'*Hey, if you can time-travel, come back and rescue me: I'll be waiting on the corner of 2nd Ave and 10th at 1 p.m. this afternoon, wearing a black coat and carrying a saxophone case. Rescue me and I'll play you sweet blues till eternity.*'

'*I wish this was over. I've never been any good with death.*'

The messages make Celeste wonder whether she would have done the same thing, or accepted a silent and total oblivion.

In the wake of the Upload, nostalgia becomes the dominant mode – even though people have nothing to remember of Earth but what they have experienced through *it*. And all those tearful details – waterfalls and zebras, jewellery and cathedrals – all of these were recorded already, and can still be recalled, again and again, exactly as they were before. Comrades indulge one another with favourite clips. And many sentimental and nonsensical phrases are uttered about Home: *The Home We Have Lost* is a popular construction, as is the balancing *The Home We Shall Have to Create*.

'We have no home,' says Celeste. 'We never had a home. We had a way – a journey. Our home, if anything, was one another, and that too was destroyed.'

But her words are ignored. People aren't merely grieving, they are inventing a new species of grief – they wander around, enumerating everything they can remember which has been lost.

'The Eiffel Tower, gone.'

'The Parthenon, gone.'

'Every fast-food outlet, gone.'

'The Alhambra, gone.'

'Every single rat, gone.'

'Every single child, gone.'

'Every embryo, gone.'

It becomes almost a game. How bad could it be?

'Every single beautiful view, gone.'

'Every photograph ever taken, gone.'

But it was only by continuing the enumeration that they had any hope of realizing the negative magnitude.

'Every pair of eyes, gone.'

'Every eyelash, gone.'

'Every crime, gone.'

'Every tree, gone.'

One common response to this is fucking. Not public, and not indiscriminate – both these things are to come later, in altered moral circumstances – but between couples, and couples of couples. There is a new abandon.

On one famous occasion, the comrades involved (all under twenty-five years old) request that *it* continue recording; also, that the footage be viewable by everyone.

By the time Abd al-Salaam hears what has happened, 83 per cent of the crew have already watched either part or all of the twenty-eight-minute clip. The stars of the footage walk around the vessel with a new kind of strut. They had performed well, and they knew it. Each begins to receive undisguised glances on walkways and over meal trays.

Most significantly, among those who watch and re-watch the footage before it disappears is Orphan. He had known about sex, but had never been all that interested in it. Now, though, it appears unmistakably fun: like a higher form of tickling, which he has always loved.

From this point on, Orphan's hands move differently when he is cuddling. The girls tell him to stop, because they think they should. As his power increases, however, their boundaries shift. The first girl of thirteen to declare she has a crush on him is called weird for about a week. That is Boo. Then Minnow confesses that she, too, is attracted to Orphan's gentleness, his smile and above all his joyfulness. Then Penelope begins to say she has always loved Orphan, in every way. No other girl joins in, persuading herself she is enamoured of the young Captain; he is too strange. But Penelope, Minnow and Boo enjoy their by-proxy oddity. It becomes almost a competition between them to let Orphan go a little further every time.

'You *didn't*,' says Minnow.

'I did.'

'But, you really –?'

'Only for a couple of seconds.'

'What was it like?' asks Penelope.

'I'm not saying.'

'Come *on*, Boo.'

'He's a little clumsy.'

The winner, if there is one, increasingly comes to be Penelope.

Minnow is almost as attractive as Celeste had once been, and is tormented by that *almost* – she is almost the most beautiful Vessel-born woman. She says, 'I hate them,' meaning those who had died on Earth. 'I hate them for what they have done.'

Boo, at fourteen the eldest of them, accepts that she is the least beautiful and the least daring. So she decides that, instead, she will be the most patient – and also she resolves that, through her patience, Orphan will come to love her most.

The consequences of what Abd al-Salaam had said – *We embody* – take several weeks to manifest fully. By then, one after another, each comrade has adopted an entire civilization; they will, they pledge, speak and think of it, learn its languages, educate others about its history. Australia, for example, has proudly, and somewhat tearfully, taken on the indigenous peoples of his eponym. Hubble takes the Etruscans, though he still prefers bird-life. Celeste had wanted Renaissance Italy, but this turns out to be a much-desired responsibility, and so she has to settle for the Roma tribes of Eurasia. (The Renaissance goes to the Captain's daughter-in-law, Irene.) Other glamorous selections are the Ancient Egyptians, Classical Greece and Rome, the Nordic races and their sagas, and America, including pop culture of the twentieth century. August had initially refused to take part, which meant that he ends up being assigned a culture no-one else wants, the European Dark Ages. This, it turns out, suits his mood as nothing else could have done – and he maintains his studies long after the others have forgotten that, as much as anything can be said to be, they *are* the Mayans or the Turks. By the time of August's death, the Dark Ages are the best recalled period of human history.

*

A month after they hear of the death, Orphan is extremely frustrated. No-one will play with him. All they want to do is grieve. It is a long time since he has been treated with such disrespect. It is even longer since he hasn't been able to cheer people up.

'Funny wet faces,' he says.

A desperation overtakes many; there are no answers.

The religious culture on board, having at the start of Mission been very diverse, is now predominantly Islamo-Christian – and these adherents are very hard hit, medium term, by the arrival of an incomplete apocalypse; if that was what it had been.

Loss of faith is common, during this time. A few speculate that if God had failed to complete the job, it must fall to them to extinguish humanity.

Those from non-Islamo-Christian traditions – Buddhist, Hindu – react differently. If not exactly accepting of what had happened, they are more devoted to non-attachment. The Earth, to them, can be put in diminished perspective.

Differences even within the religious groupings become apparent, particularly between those of American and European heritage. The Americans remain defiantly forward-looking. Abd al-Salaam is their strongest spokesperson. But it is the Europeans, including Vladimir, who are first to suggest the return to Earth – whatever might be left of it. *The work of mourning is more important than the continuation of Mission.* Among the most fervent adherents of this position are the Jewish family, the Israels. However, the acting Captain orders that anyone making such suggestions be confined to their cabin. And the suggestions cease immediately, though the idea has been brought to birth.

Over the course of the first year AE (After Earth), both August and Celeste begin to attract more and more attention.

The footage of their conversations – all those whispered intimacies of weather and times of day – had been scrutinized during their trial. Since then, however, work has been done refining sound quality, and some idea is now general about the meanings of their initially inaudible and then cryptic utterances. August and Celeste had created a cult of part of Earth, and now that all of Earth had gone, and was therefore ripe for cult-making – was in fact only available in this way – the two of them were beginning to seem a prophetic model. The paths of August and Celeste's weather-research are now widely followed, and Dorothy Wordsworth's *Journal* becomes the most universally accessed file *it* has ever dealt with. (Aladdin and Australia are the only ones not to even take a look.)

An understanding begins to develop of the significance of their lives. They become newly glamorous, though middle-aged. Younger comrades – those who do not remember the period of severest ostracism – want to join in, and begin to bother August with questions of detail. He is unfailingly polite in responding, but they always leave Hydroponics disappointed. It does not seem to them possible that this dull, scrawny, long-bearded man (he has not shaved since the day of Orphan's birth) can be the same beautiful creature they see in the footage. His intelligence seems of such a lower order – in fact, it frustrates them that he has no conception of his own importance or dignity. Everything he says is clearly intended to get them to go away as soon as possible.

'Did I? Well, I suppose I must have done. I really can't remember.'

One of the main pursuers, the Israel daughter, Becky, speculates that August's earlier sensitivity had been entirely due to the inspiring influence of Celeste. Bolt, Becky's boyfriend, thinks this unfair: all old people become boring. 'And just think of what he went through.'

The devotees return to Celeste. 'We know,' they say. 'We *understand*. Let us help. Let us in.' But, for her, and for August, the Lakes truly no longer exist – not even mentally.

'There is nothing I can say,' she says, when pestered. 'You can do what you like, without me. Don't watch me. Don't expect anything from me. I will fail you. Leave me alone.'

This harassment is yet another reason Celeste feels reluctant to talk to August: their slightest exchange will be analysed as a cult-event. They do communicate, however. With a glance, no more, August and Celeste understand one another – they are living once again in advancing, unknown time; their own tragedy, which was not how they thought of it, has already put them through the apocalyptic experience: for the past sixteen years, they have been waiting for those around them to catch up; now everyone can move onwards in an equality of ignorance.

Veneration for the cousins inevitably starts to be transferred to the creature who has emerged from their unreachable landscape: Orphan. It is accepted that he has no knowledge of his parents' secret life, but he might even so be in possession of some essential truth. Orphan is all essence.

As Captain, he begins to order people around again – and they obey in a different spirit to before. They feel, almost despite themselves, privileged to have been selected for whatever task of do or fetch he gives them. No such aura surrounds the supposed-real Captain's commands.

Aladdin had taken charge of the ship again exactly nine months after the death. But although he seems reasonably stable, his authority never recovers. In the ultimate crisis, he – and his sanity – had broken down completely. Daddy had had to take over.

Australia feels a chance was about to emerge, for him, for promotion. The Captain's grand-daughter, Penelope, is still a few years too young to be a realistic option.

One of Aladdin's first acts, upon reinstatement, is to order official ceremonies of mourning to mark the first anniversary of the death.

August and Celeste attend, without cynicism, but also without any participation of soul. During the bad poetry, they do not snigger; after the crass new anthem, they applaud and cry along with everyone else.

It is the inadequacy of the whole performance that sobers and saddens them; for such a brilliant planet to be celebrated so crassly: Las Vegas doing Venice.

Their rehabilitation hasn't gone quite far enough for them to be asked to perform, so they are able to escape the scandal of refusing.

*They are worse than children*, thinks Celeste, *because their instincts are so bad.*

And, although she doesn't know it, many others secretly share her dismay.

Yes, they want to mark the death in some way. But a feeling is starting to grow that Aladdin, who had been so weak in the past, was using grief to maintain control. Because no-one can oppose his suggestions as to further backward-looking, his ascendency seems assured. Their lives will become nothing but regret, shame and guilt.

Even in the case of a planet, the psychologist asserts, grief can be expected to follow its normal, healthy sequence: Shock and Numbness, Disbelief and Denial, Yearning and Searching, Disorientation and Disorganization, Reconciliation and Recovery.

Amazing and unlikely as it might have seemed at first, there is a recovery; laughter is heard, thought inappropriate, but also secretly welcomed: with the ceremonies completed, there is nothing more to be done – and that nothing becomes a consolation of sorts.

What had happened, although a total obliteration, was also an event with absolutely no consequences for the day-to-day lives of just about everyone. The only people to whom it made a practical difference were the Captain and his newly appointed Communications Officer. It had been their assigned task to send Mission Control a daily report. No longer required to do this, still they decide to continue with a message of one kind or another. They send briefings and grievings to the three other ships; in these, they detail their current mission status, their firm commitment to continuing onwards with the human journey, their strongest wishes of mutual encouragement. 'Keep in touch,' Aladdin ends by saying, although the earliest they can expect a reply is many years into the future.

After this, they send towards Earth – towards the space where Earth had once been – a brief daily signal on all available frequencies, including the most archaic. Survivors are not to be expected, but the Captain feels the need to address directly that absence of hope. No rescue mission is planned, even in the unlikely event of a response being received, although turning the ship around would be a simple enough matter.

Thus the Captain, too, keeps his daily life as similar as possible to before.

As months pass, the babbling ignorance of the youngest children makes a small difference, but it is the usual joy of Orphan that is decisive.

'I like kiss,' he says. 'I *like* it.'

Happiness is his default setting, and nothing can change that. The crew see it, see that it is still possible – Aladdin had misjudged and mishandled their grief, Orphan's party had been the wisest move against their collapse. Now, respect for him increases yet further. He is allowed to do exactly what he wants – even with

Penelope, Minnow and Boo. There are those who, if he is opposed, will forcibly defend him.

An important milestone is soon to be passed – almost the only milestone they have, on their journey: the halfway point.

No-one had become terribly excited about being one third of the way there. But Aladdin knows that being closer to their destination than their now-gone origin will mark an important psychological stage.

'What I am proposing,' he says, at a specially called crew-meeting, 'is a solemn ceremony of commemoration. Something fitting to the contemplative mood we will all be in.'

Boo whispers a simplified translation into Orphan's ear.

'No?' he says. 'No zeb-rayshun?'

'Like a celebration,' Boo says, 'but quiet and sad.'

'Happy for dancing,' says Orphan, getting louder. 'No for comm-rayshun. Not sad like sad, more.'

No-one shhhes him.

'I intend to commission works of remembrance from –'

'No!' shouts Orphan, who doesn't like Aladdin's voice; it is making everyone sad. 'Again, party. Again-again.'

'A party would be inappropriate,' says Aladdin, feeling the need to answer.

'Would it?' says Australia, out of nowhere, so it seems. 'Is that what people feel?'

There is a high-percentage murmur of *No*.

'I am proposing the ceremony as described,' says Aladdin.

'Why don't we have a formal vote?' Australia asks.

Support for this is overwhelming.

But before Australia can speak again, Abd al-Salaam proposes a compromise: a ceremony *and* a celebration can take place.

'Yes,' say 92 per cent.

'So, we will have both?' asks Abd al-Salaam.

'Yes,' say 96 per cent.

The meeting ends with Aladdin heading straight for somewhere he cannot be watched.

The next decision is when the party shall take place. Whilst calculating the distance they have travelled is easy, calculating the time remaining is more problematic. Roughly, with rates of initial acceleration and final deceleration taken into account, it seems as though they will be halfway through the *time* of their journey almost exactly one thirty-day month after they are over half the *distance*.

This will be the right moment, Aladdin says, at another crew-meeting, for the solemn ceremony he envisages.

Orphan is kept distracted, comrades already have their fun party, and so the suggestion is accepted.

What the Captain hopes is that once both halfway points are passed, the crew's mind will inevitably turn towards the future. They are closing in on their new home. It is too much to expect that any of the adults will live long enough to see it, but many of their children's children will: memories of them will reach the new home planet. When another child is born, speculation began as to whether she will be the first of them to call herself non-Terran.

Orphan's halfway-distance party is enjoyed by all – particularly by those of his generation; in comparison to the party following the death, it reaches a new level of debauch. People are better at alcohol, and are prepared to use it as an excuse for boundary-crossing. Several affairs begin, under the cover of dancing or congratulatory hugs. Alcohol, also, it is discovered, brings previously unattractive men and women into sexual play. If one thinks of them in terms of sex, rather than of physical beauty, they seem different creatures – worth considering, perhaps, for the sake of variety alone. The fuck begins to replace the relationship as an ideal.

The party concludes with Orphan being carried, shoulder-high, around and around the main mess hall. Celebration is near-universal.

In the month which follows, however, the crew realize that they are discontented with something. It isn't the approaching solemn ceremony – let the Captain have that if he wishes; it is the real event which the ceremony is to mark.

To be further away from Earth in kilometres means one thing, to be further away in minutes means quite another: distance, they measure against star charts; time, against their own lives.

Halfway feels like the point of no return. It doesn't matter that this impression has no basis in reality, all that is necessary is that it spreads: they are trapped; they have no choice.

Resentment begins to manifest itself; these days pass more draggingly. There is friction, as if the distance travelled were pulling something away from them; Earth gone a second time, and the second loss felt even more acutely than the first.

Orphan, sensing all this, knows better than to suggest another party. He feels that everyone needs something – he does not know what – unless it is that they want the vessel to turn round. But none of them realizes. A huge yearning arises for a home that is no longer there. Perhaps they want to be closer to what was lost than to something they will never care about. That is another waiting realization: Where they are going to means nothing.

The mutiny, if you can call it that, begins slowly and possibly sub-consciously: whilst the crew continue to call Orphan *Captain*, they avoid, whenever possible, addressing Aladdin by his proper title. He notices, but puts it down to their increasing familiarity with him in this rôle. Aladdin believes he has adopted a less formal tone than his father – and that this is welcomed by the crew. In fact, they hate him.

Eventually, the only person who is prepared to call Aladdin *Captain* is the Communications Officer, Hubble. The others go through contortions to avoid saying the word; *Yes, sir* is commonly employed. But it has to come, sooner or later, to a point where the Captain realizes he is fast losing authority.

Aladdin's problem is that although he can sense its

approach he does not believe in mutiny. The crew have grown up with Mission, and they, like he, have grown up within the ideology of Mission. This cannot suddenly just change.

But then one day Australia fails to salute Aladdin when Aladdin enters the bridge. And the next day, three senior officers keep their hands by their sides as Aladdin passes. He challenges them, and they do what they should have done – without visible insolence.

The Captain consults with his father, who – as a privilege of former rank – has always called his son by his given name. Going into the ex-Captain's apartment, Aladdin expects support. Instead, criticism is all he gets – which he interprets (perhaps he has to) as pessimism:

'You mishandled it – you didn't come to me when something could still have been done about it. I would have come out of retirement again. You took over too soon. The crew needed stability. They hadn't had enough time to build up respect for you, trust in you.'

Aladdin believes this course of action would have been catastrophic: no-one would have thought of him as truly the Captain. He even fears that if he is discovered going to his father for advice, the crew will regard him as nothing more than a puppet. (Aladdin has never seen a real puppet, but he knows of the concept from political metaphor.) Authority has become mysterious to him – how is it possible that Orphan should have any? Yet he does, and that which he has is growing exponentially. Aladdin fails to understand that it is Orphan's alignment, not his personality, which is tipping the balance. The yearning for Earth, although it has yet to be voiced – because it would be revolutionary – is now the guiding emotion of almost everyone aboard. If Aladdin were to give the order to turn around, he would remain in power and immediately regain the loyalty of the crew – at least for another couple of years. Confidence had been lost in Mission before it had been lost in him; by mimicking a position within a hierarchy that no longer exists, and by pretending to carry out the orders of his supposed superiors, the Captain is destroying himself.

'I will get them back,' Aladdin says to his father.

'It may be too late,' the ex-Captain replies. 'It is too late.'

Aladdin looks at his father in despair; *he* wouldn't be able to deal with this situation any better. Of course, that can never be *proven*, and so his own inferiority will be eternal.

The Captain consults *it*, who confirms what he had believed: the contingency plans for mutiny depend upon him arming himself and as many officers as he can. But how can he be sure they remain loyal? He asks a few.

They seem to say the right things. A couple of them, after half an hour, even call him *Captain*. He decides to go ahead: the mutiny will be aggressively curtailed.

'This cannot be allowed to happen,' he says to his Communications Officer.

Hubble feels that a change of leadership will be

a good thing – it will give everyone some feeling of purpose. He keeps these opinions to himself, however, and assists the Captain in whatever way is needed. The man is ensuring his own removal from power more efficiently and rapidly than could anyone else – Orphan included.

'And so the situation remains . . .' says the Captain, about to sign off – unaware that it is changing even as he speaks.

The most obvious way to limit the discontent is to cut off its source; Orphan and his mother are to be confined to their quarters, no visitors are to be allowed, not even August.

Acting upon the Captain's orders, four senior officers wait until the two are safely inside their apartment, then mount guard. One of them informs Celeste, via *it*, what is happening. She laughs. Orphan sees this, and laughs, too. The officer apologizes, then retreats.

The Captain's decision backfires immediately. Celeste does not even have to tell anyone of her new imprisonment. The Captain has restricted her and Orphan's access to *it*. Their disappearance is noticed within minutes.

A crowd comprising 90 per cent of the crew forms outside Celeste's cabin. This takes only half an hour.

The two young officers guarding the door stand aside when asked to do so by their mothers. Shamefacedly, they begin to remove their uniforms – knowing they will be dismissed. The gathered comrades cheer them.

Celeste comes to the doorway to speak to the people. No, she won't leave her apartment, will not cross the threshold. 'I am still obedient to the Captain,' she says. 'You should be, too.'

Orphan, however, bored with his confinement (of less than an hour), and wanting to be among friends, knocks her aside as he runs out into the corridor.

He is picked up and carried shoulder-high to the bridge.

'Hello, Captain,' he says, cheerfully, when he comes face to face with the Captain: it is apolitical, it is revolution.

The Captain makes one final attempt to regain control. He asks the crew to take Orphan away; no-one moves. He orders the nearest guard to seize him; the guard refuses, politely. He tries himself to manhandle Orphan (giggling) out through the door; Hubble, among others, helps restrain him. He shouts that he is Captain and that he must be obeyed. 'Take your fucking hands off me!'

'I am fucking Captain,' says Orphan, and from that moment, he is.


After the former Captain is taken off to his apartment, with many apologies and explanations, it is merely a matter of putting the question directly to Orphan.

'Captain, we are currently on a course for ...' announces Jens, the Astrogation Officer.

Orphan is a little confused; the yearning is breaking through.

'Shall I continue?' asks Jens.

'Where do you want to go?' Celeste asks – for she is

no longer forbidden access to the bridge, and has come up there just to prove this.

August has stayed away, with his plants, watching via *it*, feeling proudly ashamed: proud his son is so important, ashamed his son's importance may be manipulated – even in service of a cause with which he himself agrees.

'Do you want to go to the new planet or to turn around?' asks Australia, standing to one side, but close.

Orphan looks around him.

'What you want?' he asks the crowd.

'Home!' they cry, as one. 'Take us home!'

'Home,' says Orphan to the Astrogation Officer. 'I want go home.'

'And where is home?'

'Home is home, silly.'

'Is home a new planet or an old planet?'

'Home is here.'

'But which way should we be going, Captain?'

'Where we want.'

And still the Astrogation Officer awaits a direct order, although everyone is looking at him. The pressure is too much.

'Would the Captain like me to change course?'

Orphan looks around for guidance, but his mother refuses to prompt him.

'Go home,' he says again, though the vessel is his only ever home.

'Yes, sir,' says the Astrogation Officer, and begins to talk to *it*. Calculations will take a week; effecting a slingshot round a suitable planet will take over a year.

But from this moment on, they are as good as heading back towards Earth.

Joy and shouting follow, briefly.

The former Captain is dead within two seconds of removing the gun from its holster.

No-one has given the order to disarm him, and so he has not been disarmed – merely left alone in his apartment with a guard outside the door.

In the circumstances, he is easily able to achieve suicide: *it* cannot disable the weapon, and has no time to alert any crew-members to the danger.

The footage is broadcast throughout the ship, instantly destroying the mood on the bridge.

'What he do?' asks Orphan, very distressed. 'What he do?'

Celeste spends the next few hours trying to calm him down. Boo, by refusing to leave his side, assists also. Australia comes and goes, making it his business to check up.

The deposed Captain has finally gained the respect of the crew. His weapon – all weapons, are jettisoned immediately: in tribute.

Celeste eventually allows the Chief Medical Officer to administer a sedative, after which, Orphan soon sleeps.

'Thank you, Australia,' Celeste says. Australia leaves. Boo remains.

A baby is born that evening, a healthy little girl, Tabitha, and anyone looking for a symbol or an excuse to say the word *hope* finds one.

\*

The grief of Abd al-Salaam is outrageous: the vessel has never known a force like it. His cries can be heard two decks up from his cabin. He punches walls but breaks no irreplaceable objects. For three days, he sits with the Captain's body, and anyone who wants to see it has to see him, too. Perhaps, in all this, he is grieving also for Mission. His great desire to go forwards, to pursue, has lost out to negativity. America is vanquished; Europe has won. The crew are sentimental, hopeless. If he had been Captain, he knows, he would have been able to maintain morale. Orphan is no leader. He is a demonstration of wilful perversity, nothing more, and sooner or later the crew will suffer for their choice.

At the funeral, he speaks nobly of how his son had tried to serve Mission – 'in everything he did, with every fibre of his being, right up until the end, beyond the end'.

The body, flag-draped, is ejected into space. Everyone watches until it has passed completely out of sight. Then they turn to Abd al-Salaam, who has worn his old uniform for the occasion.

'I will not forgive you for what you did, so don't come to me looking for forgiveness.'

He walks out, through the crowd of them – who next turn to Orphan, but he is still staring out of the window, still trying to see if he can see the body.


The Captain's father is often to be observed, in the month leading up to his death, listening. But his behaviour is not understood until afterwards. What he does is eccentric, although not beyond the bounds of mourning: he walks the obscurest corridors of the vessel, stopping every couple of steps to cock his head and lift his ear. Supernatural explanations of this are given; the ship, his old command, is offering him comfort; he hopes to hear the voice of his dead son echoing in the particles; he is entering into privileged dialogue with God; he has an inner voice which can only be heard in absolute silence, and nowhere aboard offers this – there is always a vibration from the graviscope and a hum from the electrics.

It is proposed that a soundproof room be created, suspended within the walls of another, upon springs – but the plans do not advance very far. If they cater to the eccentricity of one crew-member, albeit an exceptional and grieving one, what is to stop everyone demanding customized rooms?

The Captain's father trudges and stops and listens, trudges and stops and listens, listens and listens; listens.

Everyone speaks about him; everyone senses his death accompanying him. Yet they feel unable to prevent it: it in the form of *him*, future self-slaughterer. Authority has turned turbulent – there is almost a collective will-to-murder. The ex-Captain is not ignored or neglected; he keeps himself hidden: he conspicuously disappears. Still, there are many confirmatory glimpses of him during the hours of darkness and powerdown. He seems to know instinctively when someone is using *it* to watch him – will look into the focal point, even speak: 'I am fine.' Never angry with surface anger, always nothing but anger down below. Even the children know he is a going man. In their games, during this waiting, if someone dies, it is always him. And their unlikely laserings and blasts come closest to predicting the manner of his death.

There has been nothing like this before; the previous suicide did not carry herself obviously mortally wounded (psychically) throughout the saddest precincts of the vessel. Her prelude had been internal; otherwise her final act would not have been possible. After her death, many remarked upon how cheerful she had seemed in the days leading up to *the day*, only in retrospect did this higher manner take on the aspect of disguise.

'We should have known – she was never *quite that* up.'

And for a while people who were behaving abnormally normally had been watched with suspicion. It was a freak, not that *she* had been a freak, but freaks (freak events) had been known to start crazes – and over the years the comrades had been very susceptible to these. There had been the wooden-jewellery craze, the stargazing craze and of course the craze for talking to Mrs Woods, the last surviving first-generationer. (Afterwards, *it* cross-referenced her answers – helpfully pointing out deviations from both her previous answers and from the official audiovisual record.) Also, and more recently, there was the craze for checking the audiovisual record – not just the interaction between August and Celeste. Widely done, though in private, was the reviewing of one's own conception, birth, meconium, first word, first bite of solids, first solid poo, first crawl, first step, first curseword. But, after the suicide, no suicide craze had ensued, or not immediately, and fluctuations in behaviour were soon passing unmentioned.

The Captain's father begins returning and returning to a corridor down towards the bottom decks of the ship – perhaps this is where the voice or voices were loudest.

*it* has no idea what he is planning – and no-one feels they have the authority to put him on suicide watch. Equally, no-one wants to suggest it to Orphan; they all saw how unnerved he was by the Captain's death. It was over a week before he started humming again.

Two boys take to following the Captain's father; standing where he has stood and listening to what he has heard. But it is what they smelled, in his favourite spot, that confuses them most of all: a salty, sweetish smell, not totally dissimilar to the krill-fingers they sometimes eat. This, although they have no way of knowing, is the seaside smell of ozone.

The Captain's father has found what he needs: a non-failsafe circuit – all along, that is what he has been listening and looking for, as he roams.

He makes final preparations – is seen walking in bare feet on the metal walkways; still *it* does not suspect.

A non-failsafe circuit: at any other place, *it* would have been able to shut off the local power. But the ex-Captain has listened until he found a sparking gap, then he closes it with his fingers.

After the electrocution, *it*, of course, runs tests on every circuit throughout the vessel – and extensive, though minor, repairs take place on most decks.

'This must not be allowed ever to happen again.'

There is a second debate on suicide, and it is decided that provision should be made for voluntary euthanasia. No-one comes forward, during the discussions, to say they wish to die, but many say they do not wish to end up as incapacitated relics on the medical bay.

However, at the meeting during which the new law is adopted, three people – Celeste, Astra and Hubble – immediately ask to be considered as candidates. Everyone is shocked that there are so many would-be suicides. Amid the consternation, another woman, Sarah Israel (mother of Becky), says she is thinking about it, and doesn't want anyone to be surprised if she makes an official request within the next week. The plenum cannot continue; smaller clusters break away.

'Why?' the candidate suicides are asked. 'You are a valued crew-member.'

None gives any answer – Celeste refuses to speak a word, Astra has fainted away and Hubble is weeping with relief.

'It's just attention-seeking,' someone says.

When they have been taken back to their apartments, a resolution is passed to meet the following day, without the three plus one – who are to be accompanied by a responsible adult at all times, and watched by *it*. (Behaviour-analysis programmes have been sensitized, and now the slightest deviation or twitch may give cause for concern.)

Assessment takes place, one-on-one, with the ship's Chief Medical Officer, Ova, who concludes in each case that there are good reasons for granting permission-to-die. She says this in the full knowledge that it is she herself who will have to carry out the preparations; the final act, however, will be the total responsibility of the suicides: they will be required each to press the plunger on their own syringe, once the cannula is in place.

The Chief Medical Officer then scandalizes the crew by putting in her own request for permission to die.

'I don't know what she thinks death is, but it's not the easy way out.'

A crisis begins, the first under Orphan's command. The crew are terrified of consulting him on the issue of suicide, for fear that he might simply say that, yes, people should be able to have fun in any way they wanted. It has to be done, though – and Australia takes charge. He is firmly against euthanasia. The crew can ill afford to lose its Communications and Chief Medical Officers, both first class at their jobs. Celeste, he would not miss; Astra he has always secretly adored.

In a series of quiet conversations, Australia does his best to put the issues to a distracted Orphan – who wants to know exactly what will happen.

Australia arranges for Ova to walk Orphan through the procedure. The new Captain pays close attention to what she says, treating it as a serious game. Then he wants to know what happens afterwards.

Australia reminds him of the funeral.

'After,' says Orphan.

A variety of religious and agnostic opinions are put to him, over the course of a week. But the repeated suggestion that, once dead, the comrades will be in another, better place only encourages Orphan to say nowhere could be better than the ship.

'I want to go see,' he says. 'Show me the place.'

This is an order which cannot be obeyed.

Australia begins gently to explain about death being what has happened to the Captain. Not with the gun, but as something permanent. After death, the body will be ejected just as the Captain's had been. Orphan says he wants to try this, too.

Sensing a logical opening, Australia asks if Orphan likes tickling.

'Yes – yes,' says Orphan.

'So tickling is a good thing?'

'Yes!'

'And everyone should have tickling?'

'Lots and lots of tickling.'

Then Australia asks if Orphan likes sad-quiet time?

Orphan waits.

'Sad-quiet time when there is no tickling.'

'No. No sadder,' says Orphan.

'If people die, there is lots of sad-quiet and not-tickling time.'

Orphan seems to think.

'Does Orphan want sad-quiet not-tickling?'

'No! No!' Orphan shouts, panicking, as if it were to begin immediately.

In this way, the issue is decided; in this way, Australia becomes Orphan's chief councillor.

When Orphan gives his ruling upon suicide, it does not go the way the crew have been expecting. Always before he has said that people should be free to do whatever they wanted to do.

'Everybody have fun!'

Now his argument, learnt from Australia, seems to be that it is wrong to make other people sad. This, over time, is expanded further: Orphan still believes that people should be able to do exactly what they want, but as soon as they want to commit suicide they stop being a person – being one of 'people'. To step outside the community of person is, inevitably, to make oneself subject to different laws.

'Everyone have fun!' is interpreted to mean *Everyone should feel contented as a member of the crew – contented enough to want to continue living that way.*

Orphan's moral insight is marvelled at. The more acute also recognize the importance of Australia's role. He is undoubtedly now the second-in-command.

Those who want to die – Celeste, Astra, Hubble and Ova – are appalled by the decision.

August feels glad he hasn't stepped forward – it gives him peace from being told how valued he is; it gives him a greater chance of succeeding, should he ever decide to go ahead.

Now the vessel is heading home, a different atmosphere is available, should anybody want it. As the memory of the Captain's death begins to lose some of its sharpness – though the footage is still there for anyone to consult, and 10 per cent do – as a new month begins, a new optimism also starts to display itself. Their collective disobedience to what amounted to the dying wish of Mission Control – *onwards!* – gives them all a feeling of greater individual freedom. They are criminals who have discovered there are no longer any laws to be broken. Of course, there is anxiety at the disappearance of certainties, but this is nothing in comparison to the sense of gained liberty – chief of which is sexual liberty.

Since Orphan became Captain, and also passed his sixteenth birthday (there was a big party), the attitude towards him of the rest of the younger women and girls, not just the original three, has begun to change. His association with their liberation – added to his all-round niceness – gives him a glamour unavailable to any other young man. He becomes, for want of a better word, a sex symbol.

If Orphan notices anything at all, it is merely that some girls are now being extra friendly and supernice to him. Becky Israel, for example. He, of course, loves this – especially the what he calls *cuggling*, a combination of hugging and cuddling.

Penelope, Minnow and Boo are furious; their territory is rapidly being invaded. They turn to plotting. What can be done to keep the Captain to themselves?

Reviewing *it* one day, searching under *deep kiss*, Minnow discovers that Orphan has never had a proper, open-mouthed kiss. (She doesn't need to ask to know he is still a virgin.) To initiate him becomes her quest, and running up and thrusting her tongue between his lips doesn't count: Orphan has to know it is happening; even more strictly, he has to move his head forward first.

\*

By the time the kiss is achieved (by Minnow), Orphan is two months older and, given the sexual attention he's been receiving, far more than two months less innocent.

Quite a few of the girls have already become bored and begun flirting in other directions, leaving only the original three still focused upon Orphan – yet three, out of a population of ninety-six, is almost half a generation.

She, Minnow, had kissed him at the Christmas party; he had kissed back. There was no scandal.

The move from cuggling to sex takes longer. Orphan finds it amusing; because he is very ticklish, any close physical contact tends to send him off into squirmy giggles. By this time, Boo has decided she wants to be his wife, meaning the mother of his child. He seems to understand the seriousness of this without trouble. Boo is very patient with him. He likes children, and slowly she makes him understand there is a link – he never quite gets how – between ticklish things and him having a little baby to hold.

'I want a little baby to hold,' he says.

Boo also has to explain how the little baby won't immediately appear – he too will have to be patient.

She becomes pregnant exactly seven weeks after they start to have what Orphan calls *slippy tickling*.

The only problem is that, having put a baby inside a girl's tummy big for the first time, Orphan wants to repeat the trick – and not just with his wife.

It cannot be called an affair, as it is entirely open: Orphan runs to her in delight when she enters the room, but the liaison with a second girl, Penelope, produces a second pregnancy.

This is tolerated, by the crew, as is a third pregnancy by the third of his wives, Minnow (the plural is condoned; they – two and three – are not mistresses).

However, a moral law of some vagueness then kicks in. Three babies by three different girls, all due to arrive within a month, is *enough*.

At least one more girl, Lili, wishes to join the harem. Orphan, as far as the scans show, makes beautiful babies. But Lili is married off to the best-looking young man available. She does not complain, and he is allowed certain liberties among the more mature, post-hysterectomy women.

As the three wives grow closer to term, they themselves become closer. The babies, they agree, will be shared between them – whoever is at hand can do the nursing; this will mean that one of them is constantly with Orphan, guarding.

He sits in the middle of their circle of round bellies, touching each one after the other. His astonishment is genuine, as is his impatience.

III

Orphan's firstborn, One, was not the first of his children to be conceived. Penelope went into labour a month before her due date, and three days before Boo. There was some suspicion that Penelope had been trying to encourage contractions; she sought sex with Orphan more eagerly than either Boo or Minnow; she was observed bouncing up and down in a hot bath.

Over the course of the next three weeks, Orphan became a father three times over: a daughter by Penelope, a daughter by Boo and yet another daughter by Minnow.

When they asked him what he wanted to call his first daughter, he said: 'One' – and though Penelope pleaded with him to give an alternative, he merely giggled until he became angry. 'She is one,' he said, 'so she is One.' Eventually, Orphan's wish was accepted; after all, his own name had been unusual to begin with.

The young mothers, despite their pre-birth pact, found themselves each focused upon their own baby. And so, instead of sharing, they lived amicably enough in three immediately adjacent apartments. They felt proud to be as close to Orphan as they were; each of them said they saw a very different man in private, in their bedchambers: mature, powerful, confident.

Over the following year, polygamy spread, as a positive value, throughout the crew. And, following

Orphan's personal example, all these babies were conceived and carried without genetic manipulation.

A second and then a third incestuous couple were formed, brother and sister, brother and brother. The brothers then reversed the trend by using genetic splicing to have a baby, carried by their mother.

All combinations were permitted. Fathers and daughters were allowed to explore their family romances openly. Children sat upon less comfortable laps.

Some called it *degeneration*, insisting that the previous moral codes should be reinstated and adhered to. *Why?* was the answer they received – an adolescent challenge of a question. From the 'immoral' union of August and Celeste had come Orphan, and from Orphan had come the new moral authority to force the turn. If Orphan's existence wasn't wrong then nothing could be wrong about the way in which he had come to exist. August and Celeste were therefore no longer seen as transgressors, but as sexual dissidents and ethical innovators. Some went so far as to call them moral geniuses. Among the younger generation, there was no comprehension whatsoever that August and Celeste's actions had been seen on Earth as disgusting, let alone utterly abhorrent.

'Anybody should be free to love, and make love to, anybody they choose – just so long as that other person wants, at that moment, to be made love to. It's obvious, isn't it?'

A young woman of this school approached Celeste, with the intention of persuading her – at age thirty-three – to resume sexual relations with August; failing that, simply to resume sexual relations with anyone, herself included.

'Thank you,' said Celeste. 'But that would be an extremely bad idea.'

An even younger generation was coming into existence, of whom Orphan had been the avant garde – a generation who had no conscious memory of an extant Earth. They were pained by its loss but it was a loss they had first of all to invent (as latterday scholars had invented then mourned the loss of the library at Alexandria). For these naughty children, Celeste was already a myth – she had broken the taboo, she had brought them freedom. She walked about as an awkward heroine, however, and whenever the chance presented itself she debunked her past – this only seemed to create her, in her admirers' eyes, as even more of a moral authority: she doesn't want to lead us, therefore we must follow her; she has no desire for power, and that is the reason she is fit to wield it.

Many believed she had told Orphan what to say about the turn, but in doing so they misunderstood her whole life. Her son had always been given the maximum independence, and unlimited expectations were placed upon him. If she had controlled him in any way, it was this: by not permitting him to believe there was anything he could not do. And still, as Captain, she expected more of him. He should restrain the excesses of the crew, starting with his own excesses.

Of this, he was not capable; the vessel had become a party – a perpetual party. Or rather, a continuation, belatedly, of the End of the World Party which he alone had dared suggest. When his mother expressed disapproval, he asked her to join in – tried to persuade her to join in – ordered her to join in. He even tried clumsily to seduce her, but only once.

Within the politics, sexual and non-sexual, of Liberation, there were many who believed that the most liberatory act of all would be for Orphan to fuck his mother. This doubling-back of incest upon incest (although the supporters of this did not think of it that way) would be a breaking of the ultimate taboo. Among the more extreme exponents of this view, a decision was made that, if necessary, the union, or re-union, should be forced. And this despite Orphan's being the Captain. However, Orphan's power was now so absolute that he could be made to do nothing he didn't desire – and what he most desired was fun. His mother, whatever else she might be, wasn't fun.

August continued with his gardening work, doing his best to ignore events for which many – positively and negatively – held him directly responsible. He knew it was a falsity, but still he felt happier amongst green things.

If there had been a monastery on board, August would have gone to beg admission; to be adjacent to prayer, in which he had no belief – to serve, indirectly, a non-existent God, that was what he most of all would have wanted.

'Plants are better than people,' he said, if asked – in the full knowledge that plants, incapable of violence, and human beings, unable to prevent it, were incomparable.

Over the years, he came to concentrate more upon sensuous particulars: the hirsute stems of tomato plants, the fringes or haloes on the leaves, the gentle angles which were like a tone of voice. They grew krill, too, in vast vats.

August had always preferred gardening at night – and it was because of this that he had been the last person to speak to the Captain's father. Also, night-work removed him from intercourse of all sorts with the rest of the crew. His activities were quite closely observed, menial and repetitive as they were. Some used the sight of him, via *it*, as a form of sedative: his apt, habitual gestures – pruning, mainly – helped calm them down before sleep.

Then the younger ones began to seek him out, the boys, just as their sisters and girlfriends (sometimes one and the same) sought out Celeste. His disavowal of any kind of moral authority was even more complete. 'Well, I wonder how that happened. I can't for the life of me remember. So you've re-viewed *it*? I have no idea what I meant by that about the lake – I suppose it was just something I felt compelled to say at the time. You certainly shouldn't be taking me as any kind of example. My life now is very simple, as you can see. If you want to lend a hand, you could start by picking up that spade over there. We can always use some extra help.'

He bemused them, and they went away long enough to think of some new way of broaching the question. Eventually, so he hoped, they would realize it was futile.

Those who saw no hope of a union between Celeste

and Orphan began to think of at least a reunion between Orphan and his father. They had not spoken to one another since the party of the end.

'Well,' said August, 'I wouldn't *mind* seeing him, if he felt like coming down. I doubt he'll want to go out of his way – not with being Captain and all.'

Yet, when this was suggested, Orphan revealed a surprising superstition: he was afraid to see where his food came from, lest, in some mysterious way, this caused it to cease coming.

'No,' he said, 'no – not going.'

And they knew better than to begin attempting to press him. People watched Orphan eat – thinking of the hand which, probably, had nurtured these fruits to maturity.

Orphan had reacted to being made Captain in exactly the way everyone expected, by not reacting, by not changing at all. He was just as silly, fun, carefree and lovable; he was just as stubborn, brutal, intolerant and jealous. The thing that altered was the way people treated him: they were more indulgent, less generally disciplinary. And so Orphan could not help but be changed, eventually, by this.

As leader, Orphan did not give traditional orders; his wishes were carried out by a committee, headed by Australia, who framed the questions to be put to him and interpreted the often tangential or nonsensical answers he gave in response.

Of course, there were accusations of corruption – corruption by the committee, but this came down to their distorting Orphan's wishes, not suggesting that his wishes should not be interpreted before they were obeyed. The King was not criticized directly, he just had bad advisors, that was all.

As the early years of Orphan's rule passed imperceptibly into the middle, with repetitious delights and incessant fun, it became clear to all that a hereditary monarchy was indeed being established – for who could follow Orphan but his children? No-one ever referred to Orphan as *the King*, or addressed him as *Your Majesty*, most had only the vaguest ideas about what a king might be or do – it seemed to involve a crown, horses, wars and Elvis Presley. Even so, around Orphan, a court began to develop, of those seeking power through proximity and influence through the capacity to amuse. Men and women were made and destroyed by Orphan's reaction to a joke or a burp or a fart. He was well disposed yet irascible. His most constant characteristic was changeability. Patience was what the best courtiers had – that and a sense of timing. It was no use trying to force Orphan into a decision, but he could sometimes be tricked into believing that he must support one he had already made. In this way, the court – chiefly Australia – slowly relearnt the tricks used by those advising child emperors throughout history. For if King, why not Emperor?

Orphan rarely used *it*, was not in any way voyeuristic, preferring to participate in events that were physically to hand. His favourite sense was touch, followed closely by taste, smell, hearing; sight came only a distant last. Music, he enjoyed, as back ground, because it was less boring than silence. At times, Orphan spent weeks blindfold – and wanted everyone else to do the same. He could take delight in the created chemical concoctions of the laboratories: grass, he loved – and had the floors of his throne-room sprayed with it every morning. That was before he tried to abolish the twenty-four-hour clock and the calendar; tried because, although people did their best to abandon hours and months, they still needed to be able to locate themselves in time – if not to arrange liaisons for the future then to reminisce about those of the past.

Orphan also attempted to outlaw the past tense, but found this impossible because, when he tried to remind people that the past tense was no longer per-mitted, he had to use the past tense to mention the time at which this banning had taken place. He had wanted to do something because he felt people were too gloomsome, weren't enjoying the now of the present enough. Orphan's capacity for living in the moment, moment by moment, was the ultimate source of his power – everyone was exhausted by trying to keep up with him. He could fuck six hours at a stretch, come eight times a day for week after week. No-one could match his pace; it wasn't debauchery, because he never seemed to suffer any ill effects – exhaustion, the common state of all around him, was something he didn't even recognize – except when it annoyed him. Hence the development of an elaborate wives and concubines system. This, to begin with, was a matter of improvization, but rapidly it came to be formalized, so that they could take Orphan in shifts, and at least get some sleep.

*

At first, Three was only aware of her father as a surrounding hairy warmth. He made comforting growling sounds but wasn't always there when she wanted him. Her mother, however, was a milky constant, and for this reason Three hardly noticed her at all.

In half-dreams, her father leaned down into her cot; these might have been night-visits or simply wishes. Sometimes, wanting to cry, she was sure he would come along to repair the world with a growl and his safe smell.

As a toddler and then a child, Three's father was her entire universe – he was so good at inventing and playing games that she never felt the need to make friends with the five other children born within a year of her; this included her sisters, One and Two.

Her father sat on the cushioned floor of the throne-room, always with lots of other people – it was hard for Three to remember a time when she had seen him there alone. He hated being alone.

Old enough to speak, Three was laughed at for telling her Papa he was naughty. After this, she was often presented as a theatrical entertainment. It amused everyone to see her dance and tumble and cheek him. The fact that only *she* was allowed to do this reinforced his authority. No-one else, not children generally, not even Orphan's other children, could get away with half so much.

Three soon realized that when she gave an order people obeyed her, and it amused her to make them do stupid things – and it amused her father to have her amused, so the stupid things continued, escalating.

If her father said anything, it was almost always

followed by loud laughter – and the times when it wasn't, most people were very quiet and some slowly left the room and did not come back. Three observed this.

Over the course of several years, between the ages of four and eight, Three's behaviour became worse and worse. She could see other children being disciplined for things she did all the time. Often, she lured them or tricked them into forbidden activities so as to enjoy their punishments. Three became expert at cruelty, although she was never wholehearted about it: afterwards, she was very sorry, and spontaneously apologized. What she was really doing was experimenting, as scientifically as she could. Boundaries – an invisible network of the most important lines in existence – were there to be tested, tested by being broken.

This was a time when all Three wanted, despite not even knowing the word, was to be a Princess. It suited her to arrange things, just as she liked them to be; just *so*. 'No!' she would squeal. 'Do it *properly*!' And even though she was only young, she had discovered the proper way to do everything – everything important. If an action wasn't performed according to her wishes, Three called upon *it* to show an example of how it should be done.

Because her father hardly noticed them, Three became arbiter of court fashions – in dress, and in language. For example, she moderated her father's taste for the scatological with a pudency that seemed created out of nothing – nothing more, perhaps, than the desire to squeal 'No!'

But then, around fifteen years old, she began to lose interest in decorum. *What is right?*, as an obsession, was replaced by *What is true?*

Everyone who spoke to her on the larger subjects was accused of lying – often with serious consequences for their prospects in court.

For a long while, Three refused to believe that the earth had really been destroyed. Although she knew very little of it, somehow she had developed a huge sentimental attachment towards the old place: she never had a crush on a boy or a girl, or a horse or a dolphin, but she worshipped the idea of sub-Saharan Africa.

'They didn't,' she said, about people. 'They didn't – how could they? How could they be so stupid?'

'They weren't *very* stupid,' said her mother, 'But they were just stupid enough.' Which, many agreed, on viewing the footage, was the most intelligent thing ever said on the death.

No-one could tell the little Princess that she had become unbearable, and so it was almost miraculous when she discovered it for herself. Her manner did not bother her, what did was her lack of usefulness. Other people had something to *do*, something that at least made them appear necessary. But all she ever did (it seemed to her) was squeal 'No!' Once, this had seemed the most useful thing of all: everyone did everything wrong, and they needed to be told. Now, however, she had become bored with stopping – life was much more interesting, Three realized, if you stepped back from it and watched what people got up to *without* your direction or interference. Never half-hearted, she was soon as diffident as once she had been pushy.

Perhaps, too, adolescence affected her. Three did not become shy, she just didn't want to waste time talking to people when she could be learning from *it*.

'Tell me,' she would say in the morning, or 'Keep telling me.' And *it* would continue her education.

After the shock of realizing that the death of the earth was a truth, Three wanted to know all about what had been lost.

She had been unknowingly searching for her vocation, and in this grandest of absences she found it.

The idea came very slowly – at first it wasn't an idea at all, just an overwhelming melancholy. Life was no longer worth living, because the idea of worth, of any worth, had been removed from life. Unless one was a great genius, and could rival or outdo the artists or scientists of the past, with the materials available on board – unless that, what? Three saw no potential for origination in those around her. Instead, the crew was more likely to regress – to continue regressing.

*I have beliefs*, Three wanted to say, *but I cannot justify them. There are things I think, and I don't know why I think them, but I can't think anything else.* She was always reluctant to put the argument, as many did, that the best of human culture was preserved within *it*. This, the curatorial view, held that, as *it* contained all known recordings of all works either definitely or possibly by Wolfgang Amadeus Mozart, then Wolfgang Amadeus Mozart had not in any sense been lost. Yet it was equally true that no-one on board was capable of playing a single bar of his music – although there was a store of orchestral instruments, should anyone have wanted to learn. And so this form of survival seemed, to Three, pointless. Images and recordings were images and recordings, not a culture – not even a simulacrum of a culture. They could be related, one to another, but they generated nothing. And to whom was Wolfgang Amadeus Mozart being passed on? Another dozen generations of hedonistic, disinterested children before total oblivion?

Three assumed that the other surviving vessels – the *Afghanistan*, *Albania* and *Angola* – would continue travelling until they reached their destined planets. Unless, that is, the psychic impact of the death struck them even more deeply. For without the optimism of Orphan, what might the crew have done? And it was always possible that the three earlier-departing craft had also decided to return to Earth. But if they continued with their missions, it was possible they would succeed in colonization. Then, once they had established sophisticated industries, they might launch their own spacecraft – further away or back to the original planet. The *Armenia*, however, could only keep going for as long as basic supplies held out: ten or twelve generations, depending on how quickly they cut back to a skeleton crew. They had nowhere else to aim for – no habitable planet within reach in the opposite direction, beyond Earth.

Since the death, the space of space had continued to change for all of them. What they were collectively moving towards, though in total ignorance, was Celeste's vision, vision not view, which was one of the unbearable poignancy of space.

For Celeste, space had never been merely space, merely empty; it was something else altogether – space was full, but full of emptiness. This wasn't merely semantic play: every point of it, of space, was inflected by the lack of human presence, by the effect or effects that humankind *hadn't* had on it. The realization of this made it seem quite differently poignant – especially at a time when the presence of human absence was so overwhelming.

There was a great new intimacy to the vast indifference of space: distance, in Celeste's context, meant nothing – and because all was equally inaccessible, equally inhuman, the furthest-known-star might just as well have been the asteroid passing the starboard portholes.

This effect was compounded by another: confined within the vessel, even the second generation had begun to lose sense of the scale of the earth. In a quiz of the fourth generation, seven out of ten children gave the multiple-choice answer *About half an hour* to the question *Assuming an average speed of one metre per second, how long would it take to walk the distance from Paris, Europe, to Manhattan, USA?*

Further tests brought an even more disturbing conclusion: the fourth generation was losing sense of scale *per se*. When asked *Assuming an average speed of one metre per second, how long would it take you to walk the distance from the nose of the vessel to the tail?* the answers varied from *Five minutes* to *Ten days*. The vessel being

998 metres long, the correct answer was around a thousand seconds, or *Sixteen and a half minutes.*

Three continued to think. At times, her wish was to express her feelings of hatred towards the destroyers. But then she recognized her own stupidity. What helped her with this recognition was the hatred: if she was capable of wishing the stupid ones destroyed for having been so stupid as to destroy themselves, then it made no difference that she hadn't killed the Earth, for she had shown herself capable of it. The shame Three felt at this was one of her first adult emotions.

'I am guilty,' she said.

Although, intellectually, she knew that there had been specific geopolitical circumstances which brought the crisis about, she also knew that a better species would have been incapable of constructing such a moment. What was wrong with humanity was wrong with each and every human being, herself included.

Three became suicidal, and thought about leaving something behind to explain why she had killed herself. There would be a logic to her act; she wanted this logic known.

Like everyone, Three had spent some time reading through messages sent to the ship during the Upload. Now, she became fascinated by these valedictions. Perhaps she could do something similar, and send a final message back to Earth.

Then, one day, she was listening to *it* discourse on the history of communication when the word *letter* came up. It wasn't letter as in reading and spelling; it was letter as in physical object. Three asked *it* to show her one, and had a moment of pure recognition. The thing looked so achieved. She had seen images of letters before but had never really *seen* them. She recognized it from the icon which *it* sometimes used, for readable messages. (Although visual messages were much more common.) Before this, Three had never known the origin of that white oblong with the three horizontal lines on the front, and the smaller vertically aligned oblong in the top right-hand corner.

Three was infatuated with the idea. Excited, she asked *it* whether there were any *real* letters on board. After a very brief search of its visual memory, *it* located a small stash in the possession of Mrs Woods' grand-daughter. She had inherited these when her grandmother's apartment was cleared out – had put them in a drawer, and never looked at them again.

Three hesitated for only an hour before approaching Mrs Woods' grand-daughter. The Princess element in her was still strong – if she wanted something, she would have it. Three left her mother's apartment at a run.

The grand-daughter had had no idea the Earth letters might be of interest to anyone. But, as soon as they were, she began to value them extremely highly. This didn't do her much good. Three simply had to say that she would ask her father for permission to take the letters by force, and the grand-daughter handed them over. 'I will just borrow them,' said Three, but, once they were in her hands, she was unable to bring herself to return them.

*Dear Elena*, the first one began, *you are about to set off on a great journey – perhaps the greatest journey anyone has ever undertaken. In such circumstances it is very difficult to know what I, as your proud brother, should properly say. 'Good luck' doesn't seem strong enough. 'Godspeed' seems affected. 'God bless' begins to come somewhere close . . .*

There were four letters in all. Three spent the rest of that day reading and re-reading them: taking the oblong piece of paper out of the envelope (each letter had an envelope), and unfolding it, and turning it the right way up if it was the wrong way up, and reading it, and refolding it, and putting it back.

Infatuation turned to love.

Although Three began with the idea of a suicide note, it slowly became apparent to her that something quite different was needed: a letter of apology.

And as the letter in her head continued to be re-drafted and again re-drafted, it began to change not just gradually, but rapidly, radically – and every day, every hour of every day, brought further changes. The longer she thought about it, the less stable her concept of the letter became. At one moment it was a gossipy rundown of what had gone on during the previous week, at another it was a seven-volume history of the iniquities of the species. In today's version, she spoke entirely personally, as *I*, but in tomorrow's version it was *We*, or it was *They*, or it was *Humanity*. Then these versions stopped cancelling one another out, and all potential versions of the letter existed simultaneously, amorphously.

'I wish,' she said to herself, 'there were someone I could talk to about all this.'

Everything had taken place beneath her surface – no-one had any idea of the responsibility she had assumed. Her loneliness began to if not approximate then at least reflect in diminished form the loneliness she was intending to address: a silenced planet. Hardly anyone but her ever looked out the portholes any more. What relevance did those sights have? Star clusters, to those on board, were as the blue of the sky had been to people on earth – why look at one particular part?

And, since Aladdin ceased to be Captain of the vessel, not a single radio message had been directed towards Earth. Hubble did try, once or twice, to interest Orphan in the idea, but the attempt was futile. Three did not know this consciously, but she was aware of a lack. The vessel should, in some way, be addressing the planet to which it was slowly returning – if only to pass it by. There was an anguish in the solitude of her intent.

Through all this, however, one thing remained fixed: what she wrote would be a letter – an old-fashioned letter – written in black ink on white paper, placed in an envelope, addressed on the outside, and sent off into space.

Gradually, the practicalities of this began to dawn on her. She would need to create the ink and the paper. Also, she would need to learn how to write with a pen – she would need a pen that could use ink. (A quick check with *it* confirmed that there were three such items on board.)

\*

In full awareness that she would have only one chance at this scene, Three went to her father. She might have been calculating, and waited for a day upon which he was known to be in a granting kind of mood, but that would have meant too much inactivity. And many courtiers had failed, over the years, by adopting this tactic: they had carried their inquisitive faces too much and too often in front of the King, and by the time they came to ask their carefully phrased question, Orphan had grown bored of them – whatever they requested, however reasonable, he would have rejected.

'Daddy,' asked Three, as soon as she entered his presence. 'I'd like to have fun. Can I have fun?' This was the conventional opening – a question the King almost invariably gave a positive answer to, whatever his mood.

'Have fun,' Orphan said.

Three smiled.

'Have fun,' Orphan said, as if repetition clarified meaning.

'I'd like to have fun with big bottles and long tubes and green-green plants,' Three said.

'Yes-yes,' replied her father.

'I'd like to have fun everywhere but especially in my apartment.'

Her father said *yes-yes-yes* with definite and growing sexual excitement. He did not notice that by saying *yes* to the words *my apartment*, he had granted his daughter permission to *have* an apartment – and to move out of the one she had been sharing with her mother.

'And I'd like to have fun in the laboratories and everywhere.'

The Captain kept saying *yes*. He wasn't really listening, but no-one could say that for certain – and no-one could ever suggest to him that he hadn't understood what was going on. He hated *that* more than anything.

'So I can do what I want?'

'Yes-yes-yes-yes,' her father continued to chant, as she left the room.

'Thank you,' she said, just before the door.

Others hurriedly stepped forward to make their long-held-back requests, but his daughter's departure had in some way broken Orphan's rhythm. He became annoyed at the wave of people all approaching him at once, and his *Yes* suddenly turned to *No*, to *Never* – leaving some with damaged prospects, ruined lives. They would have to wait a long time, years, to get him to change his mind; and perhaps he never would – perhaps they would have to live until death with the stigma of *No*.

As she walked away, Three had *it* mark the moment: if anyone ever challenged her, she would refer them to this footage – they could see for themselves; she had Orphan's permission. 'Here,' she could say, 'look.' And then, when they had finished watching. 'See? I got more yeses than anyone. Now, leave me alone – and if you have a problem, take it up with my father.' It didn't matter that Orphan's words had been so vague. They all knew that trying to hold Orphan's attention to details, minor points of law, was hopeless. When he had once said *yes*, he hated to be asked for clarification. He believed his government was absolutely clear.

The first person Three showed was the Purser, who, not wishing to question her authority, gave her first one and then, when she wasn't satisfied, another apartment.

Later that day, she had her possessions moved out from her mother's. The four letters, she carried herself.

Interference did come, and sooner, much sooner, than Three had expected. But it took a form quite different to the suspicion and rage she had been anticipating. It came almost out of nowhere. A young man, Chang, her cousin, as most of them were, told her he was in love with her. They were in the mess hall; other people had heard; Chang had wanted them to; Three was holding a tray. The words in which he announced himself were very old-fashioned. His declaration, in fact, was something Three found quite hard to understand, even grammatically. She thought frequently of *love*, but as a point of radiating energy which generalized outwards towards the universe rather than fixated upon an individual.

'Go away,' she told the young man, which encouraged him to return.

He had been hoping for resistance – that was the main characteristic of seduction: the beloved did not immediately concur. Chang had a desire for the perverse, and Three's perversity in not satisfying the desires which he was convinced existed in her – her apparent lack of desire – was exactly what he desired.

Also, her separateness made him yearn for intimacy, just as some had said they yearned, a generation ago, for mountains and lakes – in imitation of August and Celeste, who were now greying presences, rarely encountered, almost mythic.

Three was at home on board – this, at least, she had in common with her father: she accepted the orgiastic society he had established, but she did not believe she could fuck her way to enlightenment. And so, although Chang was able to rape her (as before) whenever he wanted – just so long as a party was taking place – she remained essentially aloof from him. He could not penetrate her mind: Three was so inured to sexual contact that it could go on, involving her, almost without breaking her concentration.

Recently, her letter had started to change again. It was now a practical thing: After the masked ball of the world, a note to say thank you.

Chang kept returning to the doorstep of her apartment; would not go away. She asked *it* to let her know when he was approaching, and to lock the door – she also requested that *it* let him know this was what she had done. He took this only as encouragement. The romantic films *it* had shown him, at his request, gave him to understand that hostility was far more promising even than indifference. First of all one must make the object realize that one had solidity. And a solid man could not pass through a solid door. Therefore, Three must be acknowledging the reality of his existence, and that, by extension, was a step towards acknowledging the reality of his love. Also, the films suggested that in the end his triumph was inevitable – there would be obstacles to overcome, but that (their being overcomable) was what defined them as obstacles rather than insurmountable barriers.

What Three needed to begin with were supplies and equipment: she intended to turn the kitchen of her apartment into a laboratory. The actual laboratories were frequently in use, although little in the way of science took place there any more. Much alcohol was distilled; many drugs were synthesized.

Three felt she might be able to approach her grandfather, Vladimir, who, though now retired, had once been a chemist. He was permanently drunk, however. No-one had got an intelligible word out of him for years. All he ever seemed to say was *Grass-ssss, green green grass-sssss*. She decided to wait; if she became stuck, she could always try him.

Over the course of a week, Three assembled everything she thought she might need to begin making a letter.

Chang continued to court her and, as he did so, he had *it* educate him upon the whole long-dead world of Romance, from the Troubadours in Medieval France to the grey-suited heroes and heroines of 1940s Hollywood. Three was all moons to him, and his desire was to make lunar poems of what he felt. Her initial indifference, and then her continuing hostility, were reassuringly generic. He did not give up.

On board, it was hard to achieve anything constructive or scientific during these years – the high-point of Orphan's reign. And although Three did not meet explicit opposition, the almost-anarchy surrounding her did an efficient job of holding her back.

Her father was now more than an absolute Monarch; he was a kind of laughing God, and his passingest whims became instant doctrine. Momentary decisions or expressions of opinion which had occurred ten or fifteen years ago were still affecting and directing people's lives.

His elevation to divinity had begun in affection but eventually generated fear. Comrades had once asked for his advice, and tended to obey what he suggested, but this had developed into a general belief that without Orphan's blessing no enterprise stood any chance of success. Superstition overtook the crew: if Orphan frowned upon it, it was doomed; if he laughed for joy, triumph was assured. After this, the crew were soon crediting him with the ability to foresee the future.

No major changes were made to rationing of supplies: their total journey time would be the same, as they had turned around almost exactly at the midpoint. There was no discussion of what they would do after the flypast; it wasn't a question – until they had revisited the site from which all meaning outflowed, there was no conjecturing a future.

'We are sad,' said Orphan. 'We are very sad,' the implication being *We will one day be happy.*

Whenever Three was outside her apartment, Chang was always just simply *there*, in the same room as her, and she could find no way of getting him to leave; neither by persuasion nor by anger – and when she tried to avoid the problem by going from one room to another, he followed. 'But I love you,' were the only words he spoke, apart from, 'Because I love you' and 'I can't – I love you.' Three had never heard love spoken of so often; it disconcerted her – it made her panic. Whatever emotions she felt, her first experience of each was always as a large heavy object within her ribcage: *not* her heart; some foreign body which materialized, distorted, weighed down and then de-materialized. Her concentration had always been on objects outside herself (clothes, the letter); and now, a succession of them appeared within her breast: some were molten like star-cores, some superheavy like black holes; all were painful.

The young Princess had anticipated passing through her whole life without ever having to deal with Romance, but she had reckoned without Chang. Where others were put off by her straightforward appearance and lack of enthusiasm for sex, he was goaded on.

'But I love you.'

Three began with paper.

After assembling the equipment, she spent a whole year researching materials and techniques. (How she was to regret this time later, during the years of ink-making.) When finally she was ready to begin, she went to the Seed Library and removed the long, pale, feathery seeds of the esparto grass; then, from Hydroponics, she borrowed – in return for sexual favours to Yarrow, the Head Gardener – earth, a watering can and several sunlight-mimicking lamps.

On the floor of the never-used kitchen of her apartment she established her nursery, planted the seeds – half of them – and watched as they germinated, burgeoned, straggled, paled and died.

All of this had, of course, not passed generally unobserved. But Three had her permission-for-fun from her father, and no-one dared challenge or even question that.

Saving the few long, thin, feeble strands that *had* grown, Three made her first attempt at creating paper. She soaked, pulped and cut the grass. From an old piece of kitchen equipment, a mesh strainer, she fashioned a mould – a metal grille kept under tension by a small square frame of steel. Also a deckle, of similar construction, to surround the mould and define the paper's edges.

The experiment failed. White, sloppy water ran straight through the holes, repeatedly.

Three, determined, began again. She went to Yarrow, and asked for advice – as, perhaps, she should have done to begin with. Although it would be unproductive, in terms of foodstuffs, the bored Head Gardener was prepared to allow the next experimental crop space in one of the hydroponics bays. With his assistance, Three planted a quarter of the remaining seeds. She was much more cautious now.

This second crop fared much better than the first – to thrive, grass most of all needed to be ignored. (Three recognized the similarity to herself.) Rich soil wasn't good for it, so Yarrow used a pile of earth that had already produced four lots of vegetables, and which would otherwise have been sent for re-composting.

In a few months, Three was able to harvest a small pile of healthy stalks – enough to have a second go at papermaking. But the trick of this still eluded her. She worried there was a problem with the water on board, some undeclared additive. Half the grass was wasted in producing another milky liquid which wouldn't catch.

Three decided to re-examine the mould. It turned out that the holes in the strainer were too wide; something even finer was required.

The stores of the chemistry laboratory provided this – after Three had described to *it* exactly what she needed: part of a filtration kit would, it turned out, do the job.

With the new mould constructed (Three wished she'd had some wood for the frame), she tried yet again. And managed to create a square sheet of very rough, brittle paper.

After drying, she hung it out on the wall – it was a beautiful promise; the next would be better, and the one after that might even be something she could use. There would be no problem of supply: the esparto grass down in Hydroponics was already reseeding itself.

It was now that Three began to look into ink, which she had blithely assumed could be made from some form of black carbon – soot, perhaps – mixed with water. Surely any dark, flowing liquid would do, as long as it was neither too acidic nor too alkali. This was very wrong. It seemed that if black ink was what she wanted, and it was, she would have to begin by growing an oak tree. After which, she would have to cause it to become infested with things called *galls*. For this, she would require a certain breed of wasps – wasps were small, unpleasantly aggressive, flying insects. It took her quite some time to realize just how difficult all of this was going to be, although the genetic coding of the wasp was in *it*'s memory. Three didn't know how many mature galls she would need, or how long it would be before the young oak tree would become susceptible to them.

Three despaired, and abandoned the whole mad project for an entire month. This was later known, to her followers, as *the moment of great doubt*. But the square of first paper was still there on the wall, and Three could not help but gaze at it, imagining all the things she would be able to write.

When she returned to her task, and to Hydroponics, she found several things in her favour. Yarrow was very keen to grow a tree, particularly an oak. He thought it would be a useful educational tool for children, and a great achievement for himself. The hydroponics bays, however, were none of them tall enough for a mature tree. On searching around for a good place to use, Three discovered the tennis courts and, after a short visit, Yarrow gave his consent. The only more cavernous place was the great meeting hall; Orphan would never let them use that – it was where he kept his court. Also on Three's side was the fact that the creators of the Seed Library seemed to have been quietly biased in favour of oaks – perhaps quietly, in botanic dreams, imagining them flourishing into full height and maturity upon alien soil. There was no shortage of acorn samples, and Yarrow decided they had best start off by growing four different varieties, to see how they did. Once they decided which would be *the* tree, they could replant it, in the tennis courts.

To begin with, every time he did something for Three, Yarrow wanted sex. But after a while, the idea of the oak itself began to overtake him – and then the green reality was in front of him. He tended the young shoots with minute care. Three, meanwhile, perfected her papermaking and began to study the history of handwriting. She eventually chose Spencerian Ladies' Hand, a common nineteenth-century script, with plenty of curlicues and other ornaments and flourishes. Then, without access to a proper pen, she found this too difficult, and went for the slightly later, much simpler, cursive script. Secretly, however, she had already begun to doubt what she would say. Her initial message, so heartfelt, such an expression of the directness of emotion of youth, would not be fitting, coming from her as she now was. Sometimes she doubted whether she had anything at all, in fact, to say.

Chang was almost as determined as Three. But, eventually, her constant rejections began to have an effect. That he was able to fuck her only made her emotional distance more unbearable. Her eyes never seemed to focus upon him. After years of this, Chang decided that he needed to do something to seize his beloved's attention – something she could not blank.

And so, one day, he went and fetched a sharp paring knife from the kitchens. No-one stopped him. *it* made a record of the removal, and he would be expected to return the blade.

Chang waited for Three to appear for the evening meal.

As usual, he took the place beside her. As usual, she asked him to move. This time, however, he stabbed her in the belly.

'This is my love,' he said, pushing the knife further in.

Three fell backwards, her head hitting the floor with a loud crack – which drew everyone's attention.

Most had never seen blood, certainly not in such quantity. Three was silent; it was Chang who was screaming.

A circle of horrified people surrounded them.

Chang did not intend to do any more harm, and was easily disarmed. He was to spend the next three months confined to his apartment. At his trial, he tried to explain his motives.

'I love her. She doesn't know.'

He was not executed, though his crime would have warranted it. It seemed he was no danger to anyone but Three. Therefore, he was ordered never to go within two decks of her.

Lying on the mess-hall floor, Three had thought she would die – die without completing her letter. The wound, however, wasn't as bad as it looked, or felt. Her intestines had been punctured but the blade hadn't quite reached her womb. If she had wanted to, she would have been capable of bearing a child.

Three was carried immediately down to the

medical bay where the Chief Medical Officer, Ova, operated successfully.

Her convalescence lasted three months. She was glad to be rid of Chang. It had almost been worth it.

Within a year it became obvious that there was something wrong with the small oak saplings. Yarrow worried over his four dying specimens, trying to encourage them by pouring nutritious concoctions into their root-soil. Three came to visit them, as if Hydroponics were the sick bay. One died, then a second. In order to produce vegetables as fast as possible, the temperature there was around 39°C and the humidity was high. This, it turned out, was too intense for the small trees. Also, Three suddenly realized, they needed seasons.

Together, Three and Yarrow replaced the lights in the tennis-court roofs, bringing brightness where there had been dark for three generations. Then, with some help from his assistants, among them August, they wheeled the oaks down on trolleys. Once they were in place, Yarrow asked *it* to approximate conditions in New England – cold winters, brisk springs, temperate summers, damp autumns. Almost immediately, the remaining two saplings began to revive. At times, it seemed almost a race between them, which would grow the fastest.

Years passed, and Three took deep pleasure in the seasonality of the tennis courts. Something had been missing all along from deep within her life, and this, she realized, was it – or one part of it.

A few curious comrades came along to see what was happening. They liked the earthy smell of the place. August, particularly, now an old man, came and stood, weeping. Usually, though, people found the room too cold, and did not hang around. Most did not visit at all, but contented themselves with a five-second glance via *it* – trees could not compete with orgies.

Then, for no apparent reason, the taller, stronger of the two oaks began to sag. Nothing Yarrow did seemed to revive it. He studied its water intake, x-rayed its root structure, adjusted the lighting to mimic a sky-traversing sun.

Aged ten years three months, the third oak died. Yarrow was plainly grief-stricken. Three made him a sheet of paper from some of the tree's final leaves. All her hopes now depended upon the one remaining tree. Soon it would be taller than she was; it seemed strong but, then, so had its brother.

When she first brought up the subject of galls, and wasps, Yarrow went into a rage. 'What do you want to do, kill it deliberately?'

'They don't kill.'

'You would give my tree cancers? You want it weakened?'

He wouldn't speak to her for a month, nor allow her access to the courts. It was almost as if he felt she could infect the tree by her very presence.

Finally, he granted her a second interview. She explained that this was why she had required an oak in the first place. 'To make it sick?' Yarrow asked.

'To make ink,' she replied.

Three was ready to create the wasps, but Yarrow would not be persuaded.

Again, Three despaired. But an inquiry to *it* about any other possible methods of growing galls brought hope – slim hope. Three returned once more to the tennis courts.

'Mistletoe,' she said. 'If you won't allow anything else, at least we can try that. It was naturally occurring on oaks. They went together. Search.'

Yarrow had heard of mistletoe, and was scientifically intrigued by it. He went away to do his research. Mistletoe was a very difficult plant to grow – much harder than oaks. Unless conditions were absolutely right, they stood no chance. Creating the trees had given Yarrow a taste for challenge – another thousand lettuces or ten thousand tomatoes meant nothing to him. He could leave them to his assistants. In the end, it was the near impossibility of cultivating mistletoe that made him agree to try.

It took Yarrow ten years of fraught experimentation to produce his first sprigs. During this time, he had done everything he could to turn the tennis courts into a simulacrum of Earth. He had created a proper light-rig, to travel over the oak as would a sun. He had designed and installed a system to control the whole vast room's humidity more accurately than *it* had ever been able to. And, on a smaller scale, he had nurtured each of the small pearlescent berries – stripping it to expose the sticky seed, placing that upon the branches. It was like trying to grow a cloud. By the time he had succeeded, he had long since ceased to care what Three wanted of the plant. Just to stare at it wreathing the upper branches of the oak was enough. But Three was there to remind him. Then, once it was in place, they waited for infestation to occur, and for galls to form.

Nothing happened – for years, nothing happened. (Vladimir died. Celeste died. August died.) Three worried she had made a terrible mistake. But, no, double-checking with *it,* she confirmed that it was *this* kind of oak and *this* of mistletoe that would interact together so mysteriously. And then it began to work. Small lumps started to appear at the points where branches intersected with trunk, and tendrils tapped. Three and Yarrow were so delighted that they almost embraced. (It was a decade now since they had last had sex.)

The galls were just about to reach maturity. In a couple more weeks, they would have produced enough gallotannic acid to react with the iron Three had waiting – the reaction which created the deep black of ink. But then one of Orphan's followers, a young man who considered himself civilized, and a poet, became interested in what was going on in the tennis courts. More particularly, the man – Xiao Heping – became curious about the beautiful white-berried plant that had draped itself around the branches of what everybody called *Three's tree* or *the tree of Three.* A quick enquiry to *it* brought an answer – and a very vague memory of a Christmas image, perhaps from a movie, brought a subsequent question. Within a minute, the link between mistletoe, kissing, pagan festivals and fertility was made explicit. Xiao only needed to look up *pagan* before he had the whole picture. He was delighted. Since the death of the earth, and its constant supply of up-to-date information, there had been so very few new things on board. It was a miracle, he thought, that no-one else had seen fit to investigate the plant Yarrow had been growing. Xiao, who was twenty-four years old, and sexually ambitious, had never come across anything so certain to divert and delight Orphan. He spent a few more hours boning up on the diaphanous plant, then took his discovery to the throne-room.

Xiao had not been wrong: immediately he heard about a fresh excuse for kissing, Orphan set off for the tennis courts. His attendants followed him, and by the time they got there more than half the crew had joined them – and half the other half were on their way.

Yarrow was in the courts, making some slight tweaking adjustments to the lighting. Orphan walked straight up to the oak and grabbed a large bunch of mistletoe. Giggling, he called it *green kissing plant*, and went around the room using it as a way of indicating who he wanted to kiss next. Yarrow was distraught: the arrangement of the mistletoe had been so familiar to him; he had known the angle, kink and berry count of every sprig. And now most of it was being waved around above Orphan's head. Others approached the tree, wanting their own sprig.

Just then, Three herself arrived. 'No,' she shouted. This was the first time she had ever been heard to raise her voice – at least, since her difficult girlhood. 'Put it back,' she said to her father. 'Please put it back.' But Orphan was having fun – he would not be deterred.

'More green kissing,' he said. 'All green kissing.'

This was the permission the rest of the crew had needed. Also, some of them had long been looking for a chance to vent their anger at Three, whose life had been nothing but privilege. Together, they ripped the remaining strands of mistletoe from the oak, and in doing so broke off some of the tender young upper branches. A few latecomers arrived, wanting to join the fun. They saw the oak leaves being flourished overhead and mistook that for mistletoe, or green kissing plant. Within a couple of minutes, and despite Three and Yarrow's attempts to stop them, they had stripped the oak bare – and, in doing so, had left a deep split down the middle of the tree's trunk.

The floor of the tennis courts was hard and dirty, so Orphan led his followers back upstairs to the orgy room – where the mistletoe and oak leaves provoked some of the most intense fucking in a decade. Yarrow remained behind, staring. Three had already begun to look around for small fragments of mistletoe that had broken off and been left behind. These, she gathered together into a bundle.

'We will start again,' she said, quite calmly. 'We know a lot. It will be easier.'

Then she handed the few leaves to Yarrow and went off upstairs to see if she could rescue any of the galls.

Only a couple were recovered: people were very possessive of their green kissing leaves – even as they, during the next week, disappointingly, turned brown and fragile.

Three used the two galls to make a minute amount

of ink. It was far from being enough to say all she had intended to say. Although, as things turned out, it would have been quite adequate for the message Three finally did manage to send.

The killed oak had yet to produce acorns, so Yarrow returned to the Seed Library for the beginnings of his next four trees. Over the following few years, these all thrived. Yarrow was obsessed with the idea they would be attacked, and so slept in the courts with them, the door barricaded. He had cryonically preserved the rescued mistletoe berries, ready for the second attempt.

The oaks grew; one was chosen; mistletoe seeds were stuck to the branches; the mistletoe grew; the galls grew; the galls ripened.

Throughout this time, Three left the cultivation almost entirely to Yarrow – who was killing himself with the intensity of his care and anxiety.

Xiao, who had been watching, mentioned the green kissing plant again, but Orphan was satisfied with his brown crown – this is what had been plaited out of the stolen mistletoe. When he wore it, no-one could refuse his sexual advances – heterosexual man, child, pregnant woman, daughter – not that they had really been able to before. Orphan was fat, red-nosed, grubby.

The galls were harvested, and Three was able to combine them with rusted iron to make the makings of ink.

It took another two years of experimentation before she was able to write letters which did not scratch, clot, bleed or fade.

In all this extra time, since the destruction of

the first oak, she had done very little but stay in her apartment, make better and better paper, practise her handwriting with a knitting needle, and stare out of the porthole. With the discovery of the necessity of the seasons, she had recognized one thing she yearned for from Earth. It was perhaps during these long, long periods of doing nothing but gaze at the projected stars that she realized there was another.

There had long been the issue of what to write with. At one period, Three believed she needed a feather quill. But chickens, or birds of any sort, would have been too much to ask. However, as *it* had once informed her, there were three surviving ink pens on board, two brought as souvenirs of Earth, the other belonging to the Captain – whomever he or she might be. This, improbably, was intended for signing treaties – should any treaties need to be signed – as had continued to be the custom on Earth, right up until the treaty-caused end. Three took the direct route, and simply asked her white-haired father if she could borrow his pen – a thing he didn't even know he owned. She produced it from the desk drawer *it* had identified. Orphan was disappointed that it didn't work, or do anything interesting, though he liked the shine of the gold nib.

'You keep,' he said. 'Present.'

Orphan liked giving presents.

The homemade ink would rapidly corrode the pen, if left inside the barrel, but Three wasn't going to let that happen.

Finally, aged sixty, and with no outward sign of anything important happening, she sat down to her letter. It took much less than a minute. She waited for it to dry, and then folded it, patted it, slotted it into the envelope she had created, then sealed this shut. For a few moments, she sat there, recorded by *it* but otherwise completely unobserved – and she had no way of knowing that for a younger generation this would become the most viewed and venerated piece of footage in existence. In fact, she did not share her letter with anyone – not even Yarrow, who had gone into severe decline as soon as Three took from him the handful of mature galls. He was to die within six months, and the oaks, untended, would die six months after that.

All that remained was for Three to find some way to post her letter. Very little material was ever expelled from the vessel – everything was reused, again and again. Three dared not ask her father for permission to place the letter in an airlock, then evacuate it. He was seventy-seven, but still as childlike and priapic as he had ever been. The only thing to leave the vessel were the dead bodies of crew-members. Three would have to wait until the next time someone died.

When it become clear that Yarrow would not recover, Three knew she would soon have an opportunity. It was fitting that he would carry the letter.

An hour or so before Yarrow's body was due to be expelled, Three went to visit it – to visit him. Shielding her actions by bending over to kiss his cold forehead, she slipped the envelope under his back – in the space where his spine curved. Then she rearranged the blue and white UN flag that covered him, praying that no-one would discover the letter.

They did not, and when Yarrow's corpse was projected off towards the stars, Three had the satisfaction of watching the oblong of paper float free from beneath him. It tumbled as it went.

'What was that?' asked a small boy, Jehangir, one of Three's nephews. 'What was that white?' Three was alarmed, but none of the adults knew what he meant, and he was told to keep quiet.

With relief, Three began to weep, and everyone thought it was because her life's lover was dead.

'Could I come and visit you, Auntie?' asked her nephew, in the mess hall one day.

Twenty years had passed since the letter.

'Of course, Jehangir,' she said. 'It would be lovely to see you properly.' For, of course, they saw one another all the time. And so began a religion, the latest religion of mankind – over two glasses of mint tisane.

'Aunt Three,' said Jehangir, seated upon her floor – he had refused a chair. 'Tell me the truth.'

'What truth?' Three asked, already anxious. For some reason, this nephew had always made her nervous; even before he spotted the letter. 'The truth about what?'

'The truth,' he said. 'The truth you know and that nobody else knows apart from maybe me, which is why I'm asking, just to check.'

'I don't know any truth,' Auntie Three said.

'Yes,' said her nephew, later to be called The Nephew. 'That's how it starts.'

'No, you don't understand –'

'Yes,' he said, and she felt as if she were about to cry.

'You *don't* understand,' she repeated.

'That is how the truth continues,' said Jehangir. 'Word for word. Exactly like that.'

'No,' said Three. 'There is no truth.'

'Thank you,' The Nephew said, with his bright brown eyes getting brighter – dangerously so; as if they might go supernova.

'I am the last person to ask about truth,' said Three.

'You are a great teacher,' said Jehangir. 'Your lessons are remarkably accurate.'

'I have never taught anyone anything.'

'If there is no truth then of course it cannot be taught – or it can only be taught by not teaching it. That is one of the first things your followers must understand.'

'You are not my follower,' she said, jumping ahead.

'In this matter,' he said, 'you have no choice. Part of your teaching will be the attempt to persuade me not to be your follower. It is the nature of your modesty that you will refuse all homage. You may get angry – or, rather, you may appear to get angry. I accept this just as I accept all future humiliations. For I realize that everything you do issues from compassion. The way is difficult, the way is difficulty itself; that is why it is the way.'

'There is nothing I can say, then,' she replied. 'You are not listening to me. You are not *really* listening to me. You are being deliberately obtuse.'

'Yes,' said Jehangir, and smiled. 'I knew you would become upset. By your every action, you confirm your Holiness.'

His aunt slapped him as hard as she could.

'Exactly,' he said, then bowed deeply. 'Again, please.'

'No,' Aunt Three said. 'Go away.'

'We are approaching the beginning of the lesson,' said The Nephew.

'Please get out of my apartment.'

Jehangir stood up, bowed and left.

A week later, Jehangir returned. Hoping to calm him down, Three let him in.

'What you say is the truth,' he began. 'I offer my life to you.'

'I have no use for that.'

'I offer it again.'

'Then again I refuse it.'

'I offer it a third –'

'*Don't*. Keep your life for yourself.'

'It is only through you that I have found myself. It is only through you that I, or anyone else, *has* a self. It is only in our relation to non-existence that we have any existence at all. And the purpose of that existence is to seek out non-existence.'

'That is nonsense. I never said that. I never thought that. The purpose of existence is to live – to live as well as you can, in whatever circumstances you are given, however difficult.'

'And to create no further existences.'

'No. I am not completely without hope. A baby here means as much as did a baby born on Earth, perhaps more. We could still –'

'Don't deny the purity of your own truth. Don't deny yourself. I understand that you don't want to take *personal* responsibility for the spreading of your message. That is why I am here.'

'I have no message.'

'Your message has been received and understood, Aunt Three – as have your reasons for denying that.' Reverently, he whispered: 'I know about the letter. I know what you wrote; I know what you didn't write. I have had *it* reconstruct all your writings, through close audio-analysis of the scrapings of your needle – comparing the minute differences in sound between a *c* and an *e*, an *a* and a *u*.'

'Please leave,' said Three.

'I am trying to understand the letter.'

'I asked you to leave. Now, please don't come back.'

'I will meditate upon what you have said. For a year, I will think about every nuance of this conversation. Your wisdom is too great to be comprehended, even within a lifetime, but it is worth the effort. We can make a start. We will praise you.'

'We?' she asked, preparing herself for the tears she knew were coming. 'There are others?'

'Not yet,' said Jehangir, again smiling, infuriatingly. 'But there will be.'


And The Nephew, just as he had promised or threatened, did spend exactly three hundred and sixty-five days in contemplation: he spoke aloud to no-one, he ate alone; he did not engage in sexual activity of any sort – and by the year's end, he had three followers, all of them young women. They imitated him (following the example of his modest life) and awaited what he was going to say. He, in imitation of his Aunt Three, ignored them as much as he could.

When the sect went to visit her in her apartment, she did not answer the door – and so they sat down to wait for her.

This state of affairs lasted for another six months, during which time they brought her food and other necessary supplies – left on her doorstep at seven-, twelve-, sixteen- and nineteen-hundred hours.

The Nephew, throughout this time, preached of the letter, and another three disciples fell into fascination: two young men and another, older woman – Ova, the former Chief Medical Officer. (With Three, all things would happen in threes.) This discovery had given meaning to Ova's life; the others felt similarly. They watched and re-watched the footage of Three at her desk, creating her message: a single line across a page turned sideways.

Already, The Nephew had much of a generation in his thrall – just as, two generations ago, Orphan had seduced Boo, Minnow and The Nephew's grand-mother, Penelope; this following The Nephew was grateful for, but believed he was only a conduit of Three's charisma and, most importantly, her truth.

At the end of this half-year, Three spoke to them via *it* – they did not interrupt; in fact, after they checked it really was her, they bowed their heads and did not once look up, until she had finished speaking.

'Please,' she finally-finally said, 'stop this. I implore you. Whatever I can say to make you do something else with your lives, something other than sitting around waiting, consider it said. I'm a fake, a liar, a destroyer – believe me only enough to disbelieve me, to disbelieve in me. There was *nothing* in my letter worthy of your young years. I am not a God and my doorstep is not an altar. You must be so bored and uncomfortable there. Jehangir is charming and plausible, but misguided. If you do not leave, I will ask my father to have you imprisoned. I cannot do anything else. You are restraining my liberty. I have only limited life left, and I would like to be able to spend it amongst people. I have been on my own too much; that is what I have decided. It is better to be in conversation and the mess of human relations than guarded against all love and possibility of accident. There is much to learn from one another as well as from *it*. After some time has passed, we might even be able to sit and talk together – if I am convinced you have changed and *given this foolishness up.*'

'If I may,' said The Nephew, not interrupting; there had been a pause. 'That is what makes it so marvellous. That is why it *was* a truly religious-type devotional thing. You weren't showing off, like everybody else does around here. They're such exhibitionists. Your life was a private gift. It is the privacy of your life which gives it its particular value, in spite of your denial. We believe you no longer understand what you did in the same way you did – not as you understood it while you were doing it. We believe you have moved to a higher level of consciousness altogether – one in which religious matters, seen from the point of view of a being outside eternity – are merely silly; almost contemptible, if you are still capable of feeling contempt. We love you, and treasure the gift of your life.'

'It was *selfish* – I know that now. I was the most selfish person on board. I should have been more like my father.'

The Nephew's next address to Three became known as the First Hymn of Praise, and was recited at all future festivals and holidays:

'Sweet Mother, Kind Aunt, Beautiful Woman-Alone, I feel that future generations would hold me at great fault were I not to suggest, with deepest respect, that you are mistaken. Your life was the gift of all time. It was offered with an open hand, via *it*, to anyone who would accept. That was the humility of the gesture; this is the humility of our acceptance. There can be no doctrine, only love; there can be no structure, only love; there can be no love, only the attempt at love. Thus you have taught us and *thus* we have chosen to accept. Your teaching was neither pedagogic nor dogmatic – you were the greatest teacher mankind has ever known. A gesture cannot undo itself, even though the original do-er attempts to reverse or unsay it. You were once right, and now you are wrong – that is to be understood. It is a function of your age to sully what has been pure and to confuse what has been clear. It is for us to interpret your dismay as pleasure. Perversity is part of your creed – to send a message to the universe on behalf of the entire human race, and yet not even once to speak of it to another person. It is astonishing; you are astonishing; you were astonishing.'

'Go away,' Three said, again. 'Go *away*.'

She wanted to hear no more; these young people with their shining eyes could not be saved from themselves. Three felt guilt: she remembered her sense of mission, and knew that secretly it *had* been messianic. *it* had recorded her outward life of routine, but of course her inner mind had found its way into semi-permanence via her face, her gestures, her air. Whether she accepted them or not, the disciples were not being untrue to the essence of her – a long-dead her.

At this, Aunt Three began to cry – which was taken by some as acceptance and by others more optimistic yet as blessing.

The disciples turned slowly away from what they already knew had been the most important moment of their lives – reluctantly they moved their limbs out of the positions they had, for the past half-hour, been holding.

Although they did not speak, their glances one to the other confirmed transfiguration.

For several days, they found their simplest tasks to be radiant. And for the rest of their lives, they were afforded occasional flashbacks of this all-glitter.

Over the next few weeks, images of Three started to appear around the vessel.

They had been requested to remain just where they were called up – and she was unable to take them down fast enough.

Of all things, she found it most upsetting to find herself being turned icon. And not all of the requested images were of her younger self – even the moment of her initial distress at seeing the first icon had been turned into an icon.

A formal request to have the reproduction of her image banned without permission was denied; her father liked to be reminded of his *favourite daughter* (a comment which caused great offence to his many other daughters) – his favourite child (all his sons were also insulted).

From this time onwards, Three knew that anything she wanted would be denied her by the near-senile Australia and the envious court: the only way to procure the little she needed was by indicating something quite other. It was very like the beginning of her independence, and she thought back often to those hard days.

Becoming a living God, she felt, had given her great authority but surprisingly little power.


Although few converts were made among the older, hedonistic generation, it was rare to find anyone under thirty who did not pay some homage to Three.

'We have all we want,' said Orphan. 'We have fun.'

'So do we,' said The Nephew, not wishing to contradict. There would be advantages, were their religion to be forbidden. But The Nephew wished to avoid this, so did not challenge Orphan directly.

'But it's not good fun,' said Orphan. 'Not like the fun we have. It is too quiet, too boring.'

'We will join you for your fun,' The Nephew said. 'You do not have to join us for ours.'

Orphan was allowed to remain in power, just so long as he didn't try to interfere with what he called *boring* fun.

To begin with, there had been no explicit vow

of celibacy among The Nephew's followers – under Orphan, that would have been a revolutionary gesture, and would have lost the devotees of Three all freedom. Instead, there had been a silent aversion to conception. By analysing the hormones in female urine, *it* could be asked to detect the times of greatest and least risk. Within five years of The Nephew's first meeting with Three, the birth-rate will have halved, and within ten years hardly a baby will be born at all. (Of course, until Orphan's death, there are no abortions.) Even among the so-called Orgiastic Generation, rates of conception had been fairly low – with women not wanting to fall pregnant too young, and miss out on several years of sensual pleasure.

Three began to die. It seemed almost a conscious decision – as if she were in control. But when she could no longer speak to deny them, her nephew and his adherents took over the last months of nursing.

From subversive cult to established religion was only a matter of twenty-five or thirty new converts – and, it seemed, for each stage of growth, that there was a soul attracted to that particular nuance of radicalism and respectability. The Nephew's true triumph was in retaining those intense ones who had joined early on. His message to them, his first followers, was the old one of ends and means: more in the congregation meant more influence for the congregation; more influence meant the freedom to express their beliefs more purely. And so it happened: gesture became altar became chapel became church became plans to turn the whole vessel into a doomed, ongoing cathedral.

As a young faith, it was spiritually fashion-conscious – elements within (The Nephew and those closest to him) led, and others, more peripheral, pretended not to care about their inability to follow. Image-calling, for example, was adopted, abandoned, revived, outlawed and rehabilitated, only to become anathema again – and, finally, officially sanctioned doctrine.

Everyone could sense the end of one generation's domination and the coming-to-power of the next. This did not, however, as many people would have anticipated, require the death of Orphan: the rude, rutty old man was allowed to continue not *exactly* as before – that would have required too much involvement from everyone – but to go on with a slowly diminishing court of his rough contemporaries, loyally hedonistic men and women – fewer women than men, though: the figure of Three attracted the women of sixty towards the new religion; to see someone like themselves (in years, in haggardness) being so revered was of moral use to them. Orphan *was allowed* to continue: that was the essential point. Even a hint from The Nephew would have reduced him from Captain to prisoner or heretic or corpse. This was understood by everyone – everyone except Orphan, whose ignorance continued to be a wonder.

Towards the end, Orphan was regarded with both fondness and hate. His rule had been oppressive, but not evil; he had committed many cruelties, but all of them unwitting. Through dedicated instability, he had provided the constancy the leadership-hating crew required. His blindnesses and boredoms had allowed basic administration to continue, under the protection of Australia.

On her deathbed, Three thought back. There was a beauty to the completeness of it: their misunderstanding of her intentions. She was sure, too, that she herself no longer truly understood the passion which had kept her going for so long. What she remembered most of all was an absolute certainty, and so she recognized something appropriate in their fundamentalism, their dogmaticism (although she had only ever had to be dogmatic with herself). She remembered years of secret work towards an unsatisfactory conclusion; to no-one else would she have recommended a life such as she had lived, and to her great relief direct imitation was not how The Nephew's followers paid their homage. (Not unless a tendency to adopt her simple dress among the female followers meant anything.) Their celibacy was distressing; Three missed children. The sorrow of it was long but the frustration seemed endless: they still wouldn't listen; they would only hear what she had said when she was wrong. What she found hardest of all to remember was her initial impulse; from where had the sense of individual mission come? *I have never seen anything,* she thought, *and I have never understood anything, either.* Not one single thing. *Wrong from the start – wrong and wronging. A mixed mission, part pessimism, part nonsense: I thought there were things I could change, distant things, change them just by thought, but in this I was wrong.* This was the speech she would have made, had she decided to make a speech. *Orphan understood better than me, and before that my grandparents, Celeste and August. Their solutions were more intelligent, and more compassionate, I know. People are the most important things, not entities, not distances, not time.* It wouldn't have made any difference, just become another sacred text to be warped in whichever direction of fake humility they chose for her: the saviour who denied being a saviour. She hated this idea of speaking scripture. Words were shit. Words were her enemies. And yet in some way, wasn't it truest to her intent? To speak the truth for everyone towards what existed.

In defeat, her illness worsened.

IV

'They look after me so well,' Three thinks. Then dies.

At the head of her bed, the final of the Israel family's candles is allowed to burn down – guttering at the very instant she expires: a sigh, a sign.

Thereafter, the image of it is kept perpetually flickering in that place; the apartment, in darkness otherwise.

Three's body is attended to by her sisters, One and Two, who reverently but sarcastically (secretly) prepare it for expulsion. They shave her hair, and the silver strands of it are woven into circles and distributed as rings to all her followers.

Orphan dies soon afterwards, of grief.

His is the last body to be jettisoned into space draped in the UNSS flag. Thereafter, the corpses are sent wound in a plain white bedsheet.

There is a party to mark his death, but it is very subdued. Fun is finished. As if to demonstrate once and for all their independence, The Nephew and his followers do not attend.

With the two deaths, the worship of Three, although wholehearted before, can now be truly unrestrained. Orphan is no longer around to offer an alternative.

Three is no longer around to show disapproval – if only by her absence from their rites. The religion becomes almost immediately more elaborate. Three is not the only woman to be venerated; she has a discovered lineage.

A cult grows up around the figure of the suicide, Margaret, and icons of her – usually of her entering the airlock – begin to appear alongside those familiar ones of Three: Three holding a fountain-pen in her left hand and an inkpot in her right; Three against a background of waving esparto grass; Three dead.

Some theologians suggest that the suicide had been what they called The Recipient – a female figure analogous to John the Baptist in Christianity. She it was who had been called upon to go before the Word, to prepare the way for it; that she had been wordless herself, that her motives had never been expressed, and therefore could only be surmised – this serves only to make her a more accurate forerunner. It does not matter, either, that there were no blood-ties between the suicide and Three.

Then there is Celeste, for whom no Christian equivalent can be found. She comes to be known as The Almost, because, for the generations after her, she was very nearly beatified. As grandmother of Three, Celeste is anyway an important figure. But because Three had left behind so few writings or sayings, it is useful for The Nephew's followers to be able to study the describings. These are taken as plain prophecy of the death of the earth. If only Celeste had understood her own words (and those of August), she could have become holy. Instead, she had been drawn down the wrong, sexual, path; this was her tragedy. Her failing is used as exemplum, reminding devotees not to allow themselves to be tempted.

Each follower of Three has by now individually decided (in imitation of her) to take a vow of celibacy. The birth-rate drops to zero. The effect is noticeable: an end becomes visible to everyone. Within two or at most three generations, the last crew-member will die and the ship will be deserted.

Of course, during this time the flypast will take place, and who can tell what effect this may have upon people's desire to survive as a species – if only for a little while longer. Each generation so far had shown itself to contradict the previous one – and it would only take four or five determined breeders (female) and one male, breeding determinedly and breeding only daughters (easily arranged), for the numbers to increase rapidly.

No-one thinks of this – they see the empty seats in the mess hall and do not mind them. There is greater space for the practice of worship. Already the Great Hall, previously the orgy room, has been converted into a permanent cathedral. A large image of Three stands tall above the stage and, standing in front of it, The Nephew does his best to destroy – through sermonizing – the last vestiges of hedonism. The sad indulgences of the sixty-year-olds are pitifully exhibited. 'Is this what we want?' Like pornography, the repetitiveness of pleasure is made apparent by reference to its form: the same face in the same ecstasy, aging from fifteen to fifty-five: it is itself a moral, especially for the owner of the face.

'I do not lead,' says The Nephew to his attentive audience. 'We follow.'

Older comrades, for their part, are confused by the now-dominant religion. Some mistake it for nihilism, particularly the veneration of the suicide. Others think that, by their refusal to have children, The Nephew's followers are attempting to prolong the lifetime of Mission – preserving supplies to ensure that, after the flypast, the vessel will be able to make it to another viable planet; perhaps to join the crew either of the *Afghanistan*, the *Albania* or the *Angola*. These hopes are deluded, however: the supplies will not hold out; there will be no second journey. The Nephew knows this, though he is careful to avoid stating it.

The last child to be born, eight months after Orphan's death, is a girl; she is the final of his many impregnations, and, in the circumstances, a termination is considered inappropriate.

She is given the name Ultima, in order to make the point completely clear: from now on, extinction.

By the time of the flypast, it is estimated that crew levels will stand at around 50 per cent of optimal. But it takes only four people to keep the vessel running, on a day-to-day basis.

Ultima is her father's child. She is bored by ritual, and takes every opportunity she can to escape from it.

Somehow or other, aged eleven, she finds her way down to the tennis courts – where stands the dead oak tree. After the first visit, she brings some lightsticks along and turns off the overheads.

For hour upon hour, Ultima lies there, staring up

through the dry branches, doing what seems very like nothing. People, learning of this, expect The Nephew to take action, but he leaves her alone: no-one, he insists, should be compelled to take part in their rites.

Ultima remains isolated until her fifteenth year, when a young man of seventeen, Herakles, great-great-grandson of Hubble, begins to join her in truancy. She does not tell him to go away, but welcomes him by not even commenting on his appearances. It appears that, all this time, she hasn't been creeping off in order to be by herself.

To those who have seen the footage, they look remarkably like August and Celeste.

Over the next five or six years, The Nephew increases his control; a decade after Orphan's death, it will be absolute. But initially compromises have to be made. The Nephew takes advantage of all opposition.

For there to be justice, and for justice to be seen to be done, and be seen to be divine, evil must be discovered – and so it is. Disbelief is not, in those early days, sufficient cause of death; but expressions of disbelief already *are*, for they can be qualified as blasphemous sedition. And when overt *disbelief* becomes almost as hard to find as outright evil, it begins to be perceived in its lesser form, *doubt*. Many have, in the past, been incautious enough as to express doubts – (doubts are taken as proof of Doubt; in fact, quite soon after this, hesitation and lack of fanaticism are also to be seen as categorical); and so all that it now takes is for someone within the congregation to remember their impression of another's doubts for a trial to be inaugurated. The Nephew presides. Of the remaining sixty-seven comrades, five are 'allowed to depart'. The more tenaciously unreligious, some of Orphan's toughest buddies, are left in the airlock with the choice of conversion, starvation or vacuum. One, Australia, Orphan's most devoted follower, presses the button for immediate ejection – not even completing the obscenity he has begun shouting; another four hesitate anything between a day and a week before choosing to die. The remainder make confessions, recant, plead and are forgiven.

'Justice is merciful on those deserving of mercy,' says The Nephew.

It was only after she died that people in general really began to take any notice of Three – not as a religious entity, but as a physical being. Her skin was very evenly and all over freckled, apart from her top lip, and the tone beneath was pure disappearance; she made her against-background more beautiful, as if it had been seen *through* her. Had he still been alive, Hubble would have been able to compare the mottledness of her face to the appearance of eggshells. There was something about her red hair that had been both wild and precise – that she put no effort at all into arranging it 'up', and that that lack of effort was in itself (by restraint) the greatest effort she could have made. Similarly, her beauty had been equal parts negligence and calculation – the precise calculation of how negligent she could be, and the neglect of those calculations she knew or suspected she needn't make.

The effect of all this, once noticed, was mesmerizing

– although only two (Chang and The Nephew) had become entranced whilst she was still alive. Even Yarrow had only been opportunistically interested in her, sexually. Others, to a man, had been attracted by the more pornographic beauties on board. Three had escaped their attention. Comrades never argued over whether she was desirable or not – that simply wasn't a question: Three was merely Three. Not that they hadn't fucked her, of course, all of them, and repeatedly. She had attended and participated in the orgies, but it is quite clear, looking back, that she had never *been there*. And, what is more, no-one could remember much about it. Re-viewing the footage, they can see her bored eyes over their own pressing shoulders. The sight makes them ashamed: how could they have fucked a goddess and not known? Surely her difference should have been there to be seen, to be sensed?

*it*, however, now favours her; she is constantly re-watched, for the precision of her movements – even late in life, her hips had been fluid. Her eyes, her followers can see, are the wittiest that had ever appeared on board. Searching through *it*, they find her ridicule and delight, her disbelief and, very rarely, her joy.

Watching Three is almost all they do.

After another decade, a signal from Earth is received.

The Communications Officer, Ahmed, briefs The Nephew: 'It's very weak – about the lower limit of detectability – which must explain why we didn't pick up on it before. It's on quite an old-fashioned band, short wave, which suggests some fairly primitive equipment, and they're using Morse code, which, again, is ancient. It won't travel very far.'

'What are they saying?' asks The Nephew.

'I've transcribed it for you here.'

The Nephew skims the projection. As he does so, Ahmed continues speaking: 'It's not a distress signal. More a homing beacon. There's a gathering place. The signal is a call – it gives a map reference and directions, on the ground, about how to get there. "Follow the river until you come to . . ." And it tells people to bring whatever resources they can – particularly grain for planting and tools for harvesting. Animals, too. They need horses. I would guess they've reached the basic agricultural level, and a few surviving short-wave transmitters are being used for communication. The signals could go all around the planet, depending on the state of the ionosphere.'

'Any more facts to tell me?' says The Nephew.

'This repeats in, as far as I can make out, five different languages: English, Spanish, Portuguese, Russian and Arabic.'

'Just keeps repeating.'

'Yes, sir.'

'So it could be a recording?'

'No, sir. From what I've been able to make out, there is variation. The message slows down, speeds up, pauses. Sometimes there are mistakes – after which, the sender says "Repeat" or "Ignore previous."'

'Sender?' is all The Nephew says.

'Yes, sir. It's my belief that we are listening to a broadcast from a survivor – more than one. I've had *it* back-analyse the recordings we have so far. Based on *it*'s findings, there are three message senders, working in eight-hour shifts. Each has a slightly different rhythm to their Morse. A fingerprint, you could say.'

'Who else knows about this?'

'No-one, sir,' says Ahmed. 'I report to you, in the first instance.'

'Yes,' says The Nephew. 'That is right. But still you have told no-one? Surely you were so excited . . .'

'I've told no-one, sir. You can check.'

'I will,' says The Nephew. 'This is to be kept absolutely secret – until I have decided what shall be done. If anyone hears of it, I will know that you have told them – and you will be court-martialled.'

'Yes, sir.'

'I don't need to tell you what will happen to you, if you are court-martialled.'

'Sir, I will not tell a soul.'

The Nephew turns to leave the Comms Room.

After some hesitation, Ahmed says, 'Sir, there's one more thing.'

'Yes,' says The Nephew impatiently.

'I've managed to work out where the signal's coming from.'

'Where?' says The Nephew. He had turned around.

'It's from Pennsylvania – or, at least, where Pennsylvania used to be. America, sir.'

A week later, The Nephew returns to the Comms Room.

'Can we send a message back to them?'

'Of course, sir,' says Ahmed.

'And how long would it take to reach them?'

'About two months – a quarter of the time it will take us to get there.'

'Send them this: Tell them to gather everyone together at a central meeting point, near where they are communicating from. Give them an estimate of exactly how long we will take to reach them – in hours. But don't tell them how far away we are. And don't assume they are still following our calendar.'

'No, sir.'

'Send it in my name, as Captain. And make it sound friendly.'

A second message arrives from Earth, four and a half months later – those sending it have obviously taken their time thinking over their reply:

'My fellow human beings, I speak to you today from the Broadcasting Station, Raven Rock, as President of the United States of America. My name is John Service, and, on behalf of the American people, I would like to express our deep gratitude for the action you have taken, in returning to aid us in our troubles. Never was a message received with greater surprise or joy, and never were travellers expected with keener anticipation. You are the answer to the prayers of our nation – and we greet you now in Jesus' name. We knew that the Lord would not abandon our nation in its hour of greatest need. The prophecy has been fulfilled. As once the world was destroyed in flood, yet the dove returned to Noah bearing an olive leaf, so the world in its sinfulness was destroyed in fire, and yet you also return, carrying with you hope beyond measure – and proof, once more, of divine providence.

This has been a dark time for our citizens – a dark, dark time – but with God's guidance, we have managed to endure. And with the gifts you bring, our great nation shall set even more determinedly about the task of reconstruction. Like a phoenix, we shall rise from the ashes – proud, strong, reborn. Thank you, goodbye, and God Bless America.'

A third message follows immediately after – then the two messages begin to repeat and repeat.

'To the Commanding Officer. Encrypted. Good day, sir. You will be mighty welcome here, I can tell you that. You've brought hope to a lot of folks who were pretty darn close to despairing. Thank you. Now the tough part begins. There are certain facts of which you should be made aware, before you arrive. I leave it up to you how you disperse this information. But unless your crew are somewhat prepared for what awaits them, well, they're likely to be pretty much freaked out. The world has been devastated, as you know, and nowhere more so than North America. We were the biggest target. But the place is slowly coming back to life. Survivors have gathered together, here in New Pennsylvania, from all across the country. A redoubt has been established. Our community numbers at present three hundred twenty citizens. A high level of radioactive pollution remains, and it's pretty much everywhere around the planet, as far as we can tell. There are no birds, and precious few animals of any kind. The seas are dead. Our water and food continue contaminated. As a result of this, birth defects and deformities are very common. Many of our children do not survive outside the womb, and many more are not born entire. With each generation, further genetic instabilities manifest. And then there are the cancers. These bring life-expectancy down to thirty-five years seven months. Even the healthier citizens have minor deformities, hardly worth mentioning. So as to help you to feel at home with this, in advance, I am including some still images at the end of this message – the first is a photograph of our Legislature, the second, a group photo taken outside our schoolhouse. You will see my own beautiful daughter, Rachel, third from left on the back row. We realize that at first it may be difficult for you to accept the way we look. But this is our normality and, when you join us, it will become yours too. The medical equipment and supplies you bring will be very welcome, especially the painkillers. I look forward to standing with you and shaking you by the hand. Until then, Captain, may God be with you.'

Immediately this message finishes, the previous begins again.

The Nephew instinctively knows what to do with these messages – without hesitation, he plays the first of them to the crew. He does not even bother to gather everyone together into the Cathedral – no, let this surprise them where they work or pray.

The effect is just as he has anticipated; he watches, gladdened, a selection of the locations.

Almost as soon as people hear the words of faith, of different faith, they begin to move towards the Cathedral. All of them want to be in front of the largest image of Three that they can find. They do not want to be alone, in case their tiny doubts are suspected.

The Nephew waits until everyone is gathered before he makes his calm entrance.

Voices combine to speak: 'They still worship the Christ. Even after the end of the world, through Jerusalem, through fire, they still want to spread their gospel.'

The Nephew does not calm them – he allows them to rave; to accelerate one another's fury.

He benefits immediately from not having called this gathering. Because it is spontaneous, his guidance of it seems reasonable; he is, apparently at least, calming the situation down.

'Children,' he says. They are all children of Three, and he has begun to refer to them that way. No-one objects. 'Children, please. This is the sincere faith of those who have survived. We must surely respect that.'

'No,' comes the shout.

'It is a religion of peace,' he says. 'It was distorted –'

'They destroyed *everything*,' screams one woman. 'It was them! It was them! And they're still there!'

'They'll do it again,' one man puts in.

The Nephew sees the way things are going. The second message, which he now plays, has an even greater effect than the first.

'Show us!' the crowd shouts. 'Show us!'

The Nephew has held back the two images. Now, he has *it* display them, life-size.

Everyone immediately looks to find the President's beautiful daughter. Her head is twice the size it should be, and the hair grows on it only sparsely. Her bloodshot eyes stick out as if thumbs are pushing them from behind – as if they are about to drop on to her cheeks. Her smile is the only girlish thing about her; everything else is monstrous. To her left is a boy, also smiling, with lips that are more tumour than lips. In front of him is a girl with an even larger head, and blonde pigtails. The whole of the front row is in rusty wheelchairs and wooden go-carts. At first it looks as if the image has been taken while they were dancing, but this is how their limbs are set. On display are a lot of very acute angles: elbows, wrists. Their skins are uniformly pale green. One boy in the very middle, his head turned sideways and down but his eyes looking towards them, holds up a sign: 'WELCOME HOME'.

In comparison, the picture of the Legislature is hardly worth looking at. Their deformities are almost average: vast heads, bug eyes, wild beards, shiny growths, dull-green skin and bad teeth. Behind them are two large statues, one of a flame-born phoenix, the other of Jesus with open arms. Jesus, too, has an abnormally large head.

After the howling subsides, The Nephew speaks. 'These people are our brothers and sisters,' he cries.

Shrieking follows.

'We will aid them.'

'No!' screeches the crew.

'We will go into a low orbit,' says The Nephew. 'We will –'

'Kill them!' someone shouts. 'Kill all of them!'

'We will provide them with supplies.'

'They will pollute us. We will end up like *that*.'

'So, we are decided,' says The Nephew, after a pause. 'We do *not* go down to the surface to join them?'

'Never!' shouts the most vociferous old man, before the rest of the crew shout, 'No!'

'We will send supplies down in an unmanned escape pod. And a copy of *it*, with back-up.'

'No,' says everyone.

Voice analysis by *it* shows total unanimity.

'Then what do we do?' Nephew asks. 'You don't want to destroy them, do you?'

'Yes,' shout 95 per cent.

'You want us to destroy them and their religion completely?'

'Yes!'

'So that it never pollutes the universe again?'

'Yes!'

'All right, children. I hear you. But there is only one way to accomplish this with any certainty. This vessel, as you know, is not equipped with weapons. Therefore, we shall have to use this vessel as a weapon. We must crash into their dwelling place. Is that what you want?'

Forty-five out of forty-eight crew shout, 'Yes!' The only ones to abstain, apart from The Nephew, are Herakles and Ultima.

The following day, The Nephew summons everybody into the great hall of the Cathedral and, during an incandescent two-hour sermon, reveals to them the glory of their purpose:

'This is the only perfect thing the human race will ever do. This is the only perfect thing that can ever be done – all others are happenings, not acts. We can end our incessant endings.'

The mood thereafter is extraordinary. It has been years since Vessel functioned so joyously, so unanimously. Antipathies and rivalries of yesterday seem all forgotten; every member of the crew feels united with every other member.

The only dissenters are and continue to be Ultima and Herakles, who do not actually dissent, but show complete indifference to all that is going on.

They want to be left alone in the tennis courts – and The Nephew sees no reason why they shouldn't be.

'No-one is forced,' he reiterates.


Preparations began for what they have already begun to call *Completion*; though, in truth, no preparations are necessary: everything is going to be destroyed, it hardly matters where it is or in what condition. But amongst all the crew, there grows up a strange compulsion to have Vessel impeccable for its final moment.


Ceremonially, in front of the whole crew, The Nephew instructs *it* to change course – giving New Pennsylvania as their new destination. Twice *it* asks for the co-ordinates to be reconfirmed. Then, without emotion, the co-ordinates are repeated, and *it*'s voice says, 'New course set.'

There is a beauty to the anticipated achievement of it, and a plain triumph, but also a profound disappointment – for nothing now will stop what is intended, and what is intended ends all other possibilities for event.

*

Herakles begins to learn languages. He starts with French, because *it* has estimated his aptitude will be greatest there. Next, he moves on to Latin. And then, whilst still keeping up intensely with the other two, he begins Japanese.

No-one, not even Ultima, knows quite why he is interested in doing something so antiquarian, so apparently useless. Every language is now dead, apart from English, Hebrew, Arabic and a few phrases of Yiddish. There is no-one, apart from *it* and its projected language tutors (a Frenchman in a beret with onions round his neck, an emperor in a white toga and sandals, a kimono-wearing samurai) for Herakles to talk to. Of course, he can now watch and understand old movies – but not in Latin. And he can read the classics – French, Latin or Japanese – or have them read to him.

When someone asks him what his motivation is, he says he feels curious.

Once or twice, *it* is asked to translate what Herakles has been saying – but all it turns out to be are ordinal numbers, nouns in the genitive and something about *fire*.

It is two generations since the vessel's interior has been quite so clean and orderly. Yet, into the second year of this, sense, though still rational, becomes mania: every surface must be sterilized; if metal, then scoured and re-scoured. The message coming down from The Nephew is incessant: of all human acts, this alone can aspire to perfection. And so, in some way, the ship has to be perfect. This perfection can in no way be harmed: extinction will be total, all ends over; a messy ship can accomplish this just as well as a pristine one. Yet it gives them something to do. It keeps their minds off another change of course.

During this time, a sense of mission is returned to Mission. Uniforms which had been customized and tribalized are re-sewn, to resemble what they were originally. Ranks are again respected, taking on a meaning beyond hierarchy: to be a Vice-Captain means one is united with the crew as a whole. Being is collective as well as individual.

Another craze begins, one of the final few – a craze for watching the first generation going soberly and with old-fashioned pride about their duties; always aware that they were each of them being watched by millions of Earth-contemporaries. From this, the skills of orderliness are relearnt, albeit in an exaggerated and ironic form. Hair is kept short; beards are banned; nails are never dirty. To many, it is a relief no longer to struggle for an individuality they never truly possessed. The ship's manual becomes required viewing, and the crew-members vie to outdo one another in respecting its tiniest nuances. Transgressions are reported.

Everyone has a different idea what *prepared* means. In the final months, with the ship spick and span, they follow the training manuals exactly – no matter they are heading in the opposite to the intended direction; no matter that the population is only a half vessel's capacity; no matter they are now days rather than years from finality . . .

*

224

Herakles and Ultima spend most of their time in the tennis court, lying under the dead oak tree.

Herakles continues with his languages, and, in helping him learn, Ultima learns too.

If they had been intending to go into orbit, they would have been decelerating now for about six months. As it is, Vessel is still travelling at terminal velocity, and will impact the planet at something like one-tenth the speed of light. At this rate, their ship will be the most massive – if not the heaviest – object ever to enter the earth's atmosphere. The Nephew does not want the earthlings, as they are now called, to be able to calculate how far away Vessel is, or how fast it is going. And so, in order to disguise their location and trajectory, he only communicates twice more with the President. That allows him to maintain the fiction that the ship is closer than it really is, and that it is decelerating in preparation for entering benign orbit. If they were where they said they were, travelling as slowly as they said they were, the time delay in sending and receiving signals would have been twenty-four hours. In reality, it takes them ten days to receive the short-wave broadcasts from Earth. The Nephew has to pretend to be maintaining a very ceremonial approach to communication, in which replies have to be pondered for several hours, during which time they are drafted and redrafted, submitted to committees and subcommittees.

'We are also a democracy, you see,' he says. Not realizing that this, in itself, as well as being mildly insulting, might offer the earthlings the clue they need.

The President's final communication, however, gives no hint of suspicion. He continues to engage in meaningless logistical detail. There are certain items, analgesics mainly, which he wants to be 100 per cent sure are in the first supply packet. It is clear he is asking for things to ease his daughter's suffering. He has no way of knowing that soon it will be ended completely.

Between them, he and The Nephew have already agreed that they will use the escape pods to do the transportation from ship to Earth.

Vessel had been equipped with twenty-five pods, each capable of carrying four crew plus a certain fairly small payload – plus emergency supplies.

These had only been in case the vessel itself was, for some reason, unable to effect a landing on the destination planet. In theory, all the necessary equipment would have been taken down to the surface on a shuttle. But, it is clear, this shuttle would not, in the changed circumstances, have been able to return from Earth to the vessel. It had been designed for a thinner atmosphere and for weaker gravity. The first trip down, therefore, was crucial. And, in the President's words, 'Anyone who comes, stays.'

The vessel's escape pods had been disabled after the suicide – as far back as that; their doors sealed shut. Before then, the children used them for games of hide-and-seek. Most of the crew had always viewed them as an absurdity – if they were heading to the third nearest habitable planet, and the two nearer habitable planets were in the opposite direction, where exactly could they escape to?

*

Towards the very end, the crew begin to find it difficult to tell one another apart – that is, they are no longer able to distinguish themselves from the others around them. It is a bizarre sensation which soon ceases to feel bizarre; quite beyond language and its definitions. Working communally, each finds it at first hard to remember which achievements of cleanliness are their own and which have been performed by someone else. But the blurring becomes even more extreme than this: all the crew eat together, and the question now is *whose mouth am I feeding?* The hand rises from the plate, yet the moment each becomes certain of the mouth, the hand belongs – quite possibly – to another. And the stomach is someone else's again. What does it matter, though, if all are fed? And *all* is perhaps outdated, plural terminology; there is one crew, one collectivity. The orgies which many still half-remember had been a bodily and social dissolution – yet now, it seems, every act is orgiastic, in effect if not intent. No-one breaks their celibacy vows. Sex is no longer possible – not because it is forbidden (although it is), but because to choose to have sex would be to individualize oneself, and to individualize the object of desire.

For each person, there is no abrupt moment of subsumption – consciousness of separateness flickers for months. And when the flickering ceases, and all are in the new dark or the new light, they do not stop thinking *I want* and *I will* ... The *I* merely becomes plural.

This is true for everyone on board, apart from Herakles and Ultima.

The Nephew is a different case. He no longer

needs to issue orders. He is the crew and the crew are him.

Herakles, who, up until now, has shown no interest in anything to do with the extinction, goes to The Nephew with a suggestion: in order to maximize the explosion upon impact, wouldn't it be better if every possible circuit and system upon the vessel were running at maximum? At the moment, with less than half the crew to cater for, much of the vast structure – particularly the living quarters – has been hibernated.

The Nephew nods. He likes the suggestion; the bigger the bang, the better. He also likes, even more, the possibility of bringing Herakles and, with him, Ultima into the congregation – with them added, there will be true unanimity amongst the crew.

Rather than ask The Nephew's permission for each area that he reactivates, Herakles asks for authority to work independently. He will, he says, go through all the vessel, working out where the power can best be deployed.

'Allow me to consider it,' The Nephew says. And so he does, but only for half an hour. He is too pre-occupied with eschatological matters to busy himself with questions of electricity.

The vessel's course is unalterable, at this late stage; it is going to crash into Earth, the only thing that could be altered – and this, hardly at all – is the where.

'You may,' he says to Herakles, and tells *it* to allow the young man unlimited access.

*

Herakles begins by reactivating all the empty apartments. He visits that of Mrs Woods, still smelling of almonds. Then he has *it* guide him around many storerooms that have never been opened. In each, he makes sure that the maximum power is being used. Going from place to place, Herakles speaks to *it* in Japanese – in which he is becoming fluent.

The Nephew checks up on the work that has been done, and counts himself pleased. Herakles is allowed to continue, eccentric though his decisions might be.

With four days to go, Herakles switches as much power as possible towards the forward of Vessel – to where the initial impact point will be. All unstable chemicals, vats of hydrogen and helium, are shifted there, too: it is an implicit bomb. And although it will have almost no additive effect on the impact-damage itself, which is going to be catastrophic, vast, The Nephew is pleased with the symbolic meaning of the rearrangement. He preaches upon it: They aren't going merely to damage the earthlings, they are going to do absolutely as *much* damage to them as can possibly be done.

The Earth's orbit and rotation require some small astrogational adjustments by *it*.

They will approach so fast that, even if the Earthlings are using a powerful telescope, they will only get an hour after sighting Vessel in which to try – futilcly – to escape the impact zone.

But the atmosphere of the planet is still thick with

grey dust, and it is unlikely that the earthlings ever caught sight of the stars.

Preparations for impact are almost complete. The Cathedral is ready. A full-scale dress rehearsal for the final hour is planned. They will go to their deaths holding one another's hands, in the shape of the mathematical symbol for infinity – a capsized eight – with The Nephew spinning at the crossing point.

Of course, all along Ultima and Herakles have been planning their escape – without speaking a single word to one another. It is understood, in the eyes – *yes, we will.*

Three days before impact, Ultima and Herakles make their way to Escape Pod-7.

They carry with them certain meaningful objects, hastily gathered: the first page of experimental paper made by Three, one of Orphan's pieces of wooden jewellery, the four letters from Earth, the tea-caddy, a test-tube containing the preserved yellow-grey dust of a tennis ball; they bring clothes for warm and cold weather. The rest of the survival equipment, they trust, will already be on board.

Herakles has sufficient authority to power up the pods, and they are in full working order.

It takes them three minutes to get inside, seal the door and strap themselves in. Throughout, Herakles uses a mixture of French, Latin and Japanese to speak to *it* – his motive, at least, revealed. No-one watching can possibly understand.

Ultima, during even these hurried moments, has

been able to look out of the window and see the home planet, grey beneath cloud.

The escape pod, at the second it detaches, keeps a full copy of *it* and of all *it*'s knowledge – upon which we have based our account of the UNSS *Armenia*.

Herakles nods, and Ultima pulls the lever which frees them.

Once away, they send a message: 'We could not prevent you but we could not join you . . .'

The Nephew has always preached that there is no compulsion about the religion of Three – and so, even in his fury at the lovers' escape, he cannot admit that escape is what it was, nor that he feels furious.

'We must concentrate upon what is ahead,' he says. 'Glory awaits. What we do is such a clean thing, so necessary, such a prophylactic against universal disaster.'

The last three days on board are all ceremonial.

At the start of the final hour, the crew rise to their feet and begin to shriek. If they feel terror, it is only terror that their mission might not be accomplished. In the death of their religion will be the death of another religion.

The earth, when it appears within the projection, grows rapidly in size. Upon either side of it stand images of Three, one from her birth, one from her deathbed. There are only minutes left.

The fascination grows, along with the panic.

The Nephew makes his final broadcast to the President.

'We bring punishment. The death of the earth was caused by spiritual greed – the desire for meaningless territorial domination. We have no territory. We have never had territory. We have space, and now we bring it home to you. We do not expect repentance, merely knowledge. Everything you did was wrong. This time, there will be no resurrection. We will destroy you completely, finishing the job you could not accomplish. We will destroy your prophet.'

Then he shuts down all channels. If there is to be a response, he does not wish to hear it – nor have the crew hear it. Though there is absolutely nothing they could do. Even to explode the ship before it enters Earth's atmosphere will not save those down below.

The Nephew can imagine the response the President will give – calm defiance, faith in the Lord. He knows that he, in the same circumstances, would say something almost identical.

The ultimate moments are to be spent by each of them in silent prayer. Before then, he makes a final sermon:

'And so we come to completion. Please don't expect me to say anything new or startling to you. There is nothing new or startling to be said. This is the end. I am used up. You are used up. We are all of us used up. I could say that it was all a joke. That I won. It is true that my own secret suicidal impulses are about to be fulfilled. Is it possible that a man, because he wanted so much to die myself – I mean, himself – is it possible he would be prepared to kill not only his friends, his family, his crew, but his species? I can only leave you to judge that for yourselves. No, that is untrue. I will not leave you at all. I will be together with you, whatever happens.'

Three had sent a letter, on their behalf; there was no reason for them to continue to exist.

Down through the dark atmosphere plunges the million-tonne vessel. It has been constructed in space, and never intended to withstand such gravitational forces. The final records we have show the shearing away of vast sections of the superstructure. The main length of the core breaks off at an early stage of the descent. It is estimated that, by the time of the impact, the vessel had separated into ten discrete fragments. These fell within a fifty-kilometre radius. Most of the damage would have been caused by the generator core – although Herakles' primed nose section would also have been extremely combustible.

Through luck mainly, it seems, two of the largest sections fell directly on to New Pennsylvania – where the awaiting crowds of the defective and disfigured were incinerated in under a second.

Before this, however, they would have had perhaps two minutes of falling knowledge during which to panic and pray.

Excavations of the site show that many of the children died embracing one another, and yet others down upon their knees.

The extinction proved completely successful, from The Nephew's point of view – no-one either inside or outside the blast zone survived. The planet was dead.

V

Herakles and Ultima lived a remarkably calm, civilized life within the pod. What it recalled was nothing so much as Celeste and August's early days laid out on the tennis courts, before sex.

Once it became clear that the atmosphere of Earth was so full of debris from the *Armenia* that no descent could safely be made, the two of them grieved for their lost futures. Then they set the pod in a high, stable orbit, from whence they had a good view of the dark-spewing clouds of the planet – and spent the time before their oxygen ran out, and they asphyxiated, in conversation.

In ten months, the time allotted to them, they managed – just about – to recapitulate the whole of human history. They were not interested in anything other than that, the human. Mathematics, physics, chemistry and zoology came into the account they required of *it*, but only for the effects they had upon humanity. The truths discovered, about plants or planets, were omitted unless they made for a definite difference. Herakles and Ultima read, listened, watched and, more often still, asked. It was good to have *it* with them – the same old voice.

History, in the retelling, progressed. At first they were fascinated, later they were appalled, disgusted and ashamed – though, personally, their lives had been largely without blame.

'It was inevitable,' said Herakles, around 1500BC

This conviction, once uttered, could only flourish. The twentieth century, despite its reputation, didn't even appear exceptional, culminatory; the twenty-first century, in retrospect, was a foregone conclusion.

'There wasn't any other end,' said Ultima.

Herakles agreed: 'The big surprise is, it took so long.'

'Stupid,' said Ultima. 'So stupid.'

'Yes,' said Herakles, then said no more. There was no more to say. Besides, they were starting to run out of oxygen, and speech used up a few more cc's than calm silence.

They had no formal *describe*, as had their ancestors, but they moved through a whole universe of invention and speculation.

A favourite topic was what they *would have done*, had they been born on Earth around the time the vessel departed. Herakles was realistic – perhaps he wouldn't have been lucky enough to have any choice; perhaps he would have been stuck on a mountain farm with difficult soil and difficult parents; perhaps he would have been a slum-child. Ultima allowed herself total freedom – and eventually persuaded Herakles to join her in the game.

'I would have been an opera singer,' she said, one day. I would have stood in the strong light on stage, and everyone would have clapped me. For hours and hours.' And then, a few weeks later, 'I would have been an architect and designed the tallest building in the world. But I would have made it feel intimate, like a plant.' Later still, it was, 'I would have had twelve children and raised them to make the world a better place. Between them, they could have done it. Twelve people can achieve anything.'

The game continued, a broken conversation:

'I would have gone to the highest part of the mountains,' said Ultima. 'I could not have lived, knowing those places were there and that I hadn't ever been up them. But also, I would have gone to the deepest bottom of the sea, and for the same reason.'

Said Herakles, 'I would have been a physicist, then, and designed a faster engine to get to new planets in less time.'

'I would have been a writer on paper, with a proper pen, like Three, but writing stories, to take people far away in an instant.'

'I would have been a failure,' Herakles said, 'an addict of failure.'

'Then I would have been a prostitute, fucking anyone who came along, however ugly and diseased they were. I would have tried to be kind to them.'

Ultima said, 'I would have made people understand one another better. I would have gone on a mission to Jerusalem and explained why everybody should just relax and live in peace because – underneath their differences – they all believed the same thing as each other, really. They believed in God, who didn't want what happened to happen.'

'I would have been an assassin, killing anyone I thought was going to kill more than a hundred people. The world would have been a better place.'

'There was never a successful murder on board,' said Ultima, as an aside. 'Isn't that strange? But you would never have been that, a killer. You would have been captain of a boat.'

'I wasn't going to be Captain of Vessel.'

'The sea is different to space. You would have been better on the sea. Or you would have been a monk.'

The game now turned around.

'You would have cleaned things,' said Herakles. 'You would have tried to make everything a little nicer than when you found it. You would have found the right places for things – putting them where they fitted with what was around and beside them.'

'I'm sure you would have been a doctor, making people feel better.'

'Perhaps I would,' said Herakles. 'You like me more than I do.'

'I would have been a midwife, helping babies through the difficult business of getting born, bringing wonderful and boring and terrifying new people out into the world.'

'I would have written as many books as I could, just so there were more books after I died than before I was born.'

'I would have read the same book again and again and again and again,' said Herakles, 'until I knew the words in it so well I didn't even have to look at them to read them.'

*

'I would have been a very fast runner who didn't stop running even when the race was over.'

'I would have stood in one place and seen how it changed all through my life, making notes as time passed.'
    'I would have done exactly the same, but I wouldn't have stood, I would have sat.'
    'Then you would have fallen asleep sometimes,' said Ultima.
    'Yes, when it got boring or late. There's no problem admitting that things sometimes get boring to watch.'

'I would have made copies of natural things, like trees. I would have studied them extremely closely, and transmitted them to another medium – '
    'There was a name for that,' said Herakles.
    'An artist?'
    'No, for making things about things.'
    'I would have ended up just by pointing at things and saying, "I didn't make that – that tree – but, if I could have done I would have done."'
    'I would have tried to find you, so that I could hear you say things just like that. To be with someone as wonderful as you, and listen to the things only you would say, that would have been enough for me.'
    'But you can do that now,' said Ultima.
    'I can.'
    'And I would have said different things then.'
    'I suppose so.'
    'And I would have been a different person.'

'If you'd been a different person, I'd have found the other one, the one who was you now.'

'How?' Ultima asked.

'I have a sense.'

'What do you mean?'

'I have a sense of you,' said Herakles.

'I know what you mean. I'm just teasing you.'

'Don't. It hurts me to think you don't know – even for a moment. That could be the moment I die.'

There had been no hope, not for one moment, but four months into their wait, Ultima conceived. It would, we know, have been a baby boy.

The two of them discussed what they would have called it: August or Zack or Robin or James, May or June or Marnie or Nova. Anything but Eve or Adam, on that they were agreed.

At the time of their deaths, they had come to no final decision.

They didn't want to die, not even right at the hallucinating, lung-painful end; they wanted as much of life, with one another, in one another's sight, as possible. And so, although they also wanted to unite physically one final time, they held back: it – the gasping moments of it – would shorten their conscious love by perhaps half an hour. Better, really, to gaze.

Their remains were discovered in the pod, when we returned; utterly undecayed. They had before they died given *it* an order: *Once you observe both our bodies to be without heartbeats for a whole hour, gently render the capsule airless.* But that story is too well known to bear repeating.

Green was the earth below, from equator to pole. Uninhabitable, however. Not for another thousand years, at least. We will wait.

# TOBY LITT

**GHOST STORY**

Agatha and Paddy were to have a baby. They bought a new house on the south coast. But then something happened and they found they couldn't fill their new home – no matter how they tried. That emptiness threatened their relationship, and they began to ask: how was it they could be haunted by something that had never existed?

'Unsettling, extraordinarily vivid . . . makes you remember what reading's all about' *Daily Telegraph*

'One of the most compelling books of the year. Litt's finest novel so far' Ali Smith, *The Times Literary Supplement*

'Beautifully written, moves and intrigues and cracks along at a galloping pace. A striking portrayal of how bereavement can overshadow life' *Guardian*

# TOBY LITT

**HOSPITAL**

The end of the world doesn't come with a bang or a whimper, but with the chukka-chukka of a helicopter coming into land . . .

*Hospital* is about blue murder and saving lives, having sex and surgery, falling in love and falling from a great height, crazy voodoo and hypnotic surveillance – it's about the last days and the first days. And the Rubber Nurse knows you've been very naughty and is going to teach you a well-deserved lesson.

It's the story of a lost boy wandering the corridors of a strange, antiseptic building, looking and hoping for a chance to get home. And also of a man who won't wake up despite the best efforts of the hospital staff – and while he sleeps, a threatening darkness settles over everything . . .

'Litt has created an extraordinarily vivid comic nightmare, an apocalyptic vision for our own weird times' *Guardian*

'A mind-bending trip – like a shot of morphine . . . a dark, absurd fairytale . . . an epic nightmare' *London Lite*

'Vivid, hallucinatory, startling and humane. Defibrillating fiction' China Mieville

# He just wanted a decent book to read ...

Not too much to ask, is it? It was in 1935 when Allen Lane, Managing Director of Bodley Head Publishers, stood on a platform at Exeter railway station looking for something good to read on his journey back to London. His choice was limited to popular magazines and poor-quality paperbacks – the same choice faced every day by the vast majority of readers, few of whom could afford hardbacks. Lane's disappointment and subsequent anger at the range of books generally available led him to found a company – and change the world.

*'We believed in the existence in this country of a vast reading public for intelligent books at a low price, and staked everything on it'*
**Sir Allen Lane, 1902–1970, founder of Penguin Books**

The quality paperback had arrived – and not just in bookshops. Lane was adamant that his Penguins should appear in chain stores and tobacconists, and should cost no more than a packet of cigarettes.

Reading habits (and cigarette prices) have changed since 1935, but Penguin still believes in publishing the best books for everybody to enjoy. We still believe that good design costs no more than bad design, and we still believe that quality books published passionately and responsibly make the world a better place.

So wherever you see the little bird – whether it's on a piece of prize-winning literary fiction or a celebrity autobiography, political tour de force or historical masterpiece, a serial-killer thriller, reference book, world classic or a piece of pure escapism – you can bet that it represents the very best that the genre has to offer.

## Whatever you like to read – trust Penguin.